Heaven:

The Adventure Begins

Jonathan Stone and the Kingdom

Novel by A. R. Duprey

ISBN 978-1-940982-05-2

Media 14:36, Inc.
PO Box 477
Agawam,   MA   01001
http://Media1436.com
GoodChristianMovies.com

Alan Duprey © Copyright
Registration: 2011925247
All rights reserved
Printed in the United States of America

Alan Duprey

Email: alanduprey@yahoo.com

1 Corinthians 2:9-10

"No eye has seen, no ear has heard,
no mind has conceived what God
has prepared for those who love him.
These are the things God has revealed
to us by his Spirit."

Introduction:

This story was written out of the obedience that comes from faith. It was not my desire to begin this venture, and it was only completed by the God who directs the steps of His people. I pray that this book will be a blessing to the Church of the Living God, and that through these pages the glory of Christ may shine brightly into the hearts of the readers.

I would like to personally thank my wife, Jennie, for the love, encouragement, support and blessings she brings to my life and the lives of so many others. I would also like to thank my children, Tom and Jenal, for being the children I always dreamed of having. I cannot thank God enough for his faithfulness in my family; I am truly blessed beyond measure.

I would like to thank the rest of my family for their love and support. I praise God that He has put me in a family that loves each other and truly enjoys each other's company. I look forward to seeing the fingerprints of God's hands on each of our lives.

I would like to thank my pastor, Emmanuel Haqq, for his faithful preaching and the love he has for the people under his care. I would like to thank Rusty and Mary Annis, Dave Fritsch and many others for their direction and guidance in this endeavor. I would also like to thank the many people who encouraged me to move forward in the completion of this book.

Now to him who is able to do immeasurably more than all we ask or imagine, according to his power that is at work within us, to him be glory in the church and in Christ Jesus throughout all generations, forever and ever! Amen…. Ephesians 3:20-21

Contents

Foreword

Who would have ever believed or expected that God could use a lowly man to write a book on such a grand subject? It is truly God's grace that moved me, a man with no desire or ability for writing, to complete this book. God had to work the clay and move His hands over the pottery of my life to enable me to begin and finish this project.

Chapter one is not where the story began. It started near the end of the year 2007 at Dwight Chapel in Belchertown, MA on a Sunday morning. I was at church listening to a sermon on the resurrection of Jesus Christ from the dead. One point that stood out was that Jesus appeared to His disciples after the resurrection. These appearances showed that He knew them, loved them and wanted to be with them. One of the main points I drew from the sermon was that Jesus was showing us that our earthly relationships continue on into eternity.

In the middle of the sermon, the Holy Spirit spoke to me. I cannot say I heard a verbal command, but deep within my being I heard the words, "I want you to write a book about this subject; I want you to write about heaven." All through the sermon the voice spoke deep within me. I tried to suppress the voice and said, "This is all in my head; it's me talking, not God." The voice continued on and on saying, "I want you to write a book about heaven."

It did not stop there, but continued throughout the day and into the days and weeks to come. I had no desire to write a book. I didn't even like writing of any type. I prefer talking on the phone or in person. I have never heard a study or sermon about heaven, but I had some ideas what heaven was like from studying the Scriptures. However, I had never immersed myself deeply into the subject. But the voice continued telling me to write, write and write.

The voice continued for the next month or two. I tried to suppress the voice because I did not know if it was coming from me or if it was truly the Lord's calling. One day I was at work and during lunch I wanted to settle the matter once and for all. I decided to write one page. I spent about forty minutes writing the first page with no thought or direction. After this, I showed it to a couple of co-workers, including my brother, Brian Duprey, and Dave Matuszek, and asked them for their opinion. After reading it, they said it was really good and wanted to hear what would happen next in the story. This was a surprise, so I wrote the next page and showed it to them. They both agreed that I should continue.

At this point I decided to commit to write one chapter, which was two and a half pages long. I decided to email it to my pastor to get another opinion. Here is the original email, dated Sunday January 20, 2008. I kept the email as originally sent, so the reader will get an idea of where I was in my writing.

Hi Emmanuel, this is what I got so far, email me back if you have any suggestions or comments. I have no real direction I am going in just toying as stuff comes in my mind. Don't worry about grammar etc., context only Email me back at work

After he read the first chapter, I met with him. He basically said, "Alan, this is surprising. I never would have expected this would come from you." (He can say that, because he knows me). He continued, "The Lord may be bringing forward a gift of writing in you; I think you should continue with the book."

So, the book began with a little wind behind the sails. One of the problems which I had was that I had no idea or direction on what to write. I never knew what the next paragraph was going to say, never mind let alone the next chapter. Someone said, write an outline of the book and then begin to write it. Another person said to create a tension in heaven and write about that. None of these things were pursued because I am not organized in any way.

Each chapter came into being by hearing a sermon or reading something in the Scriptures and that same voice which inspired me to begin writing would say, "I want you to write about this."

I looked for help and direction, but God seemed to continually close every door. I tried to get help from various people, but they all fell through because of other commitments, and possibly because I wasn't persistent. I was looking for someone who would allow me to write and breathe life into the story while they would correct it grammatically. I did not find anyone who was able to walk alongside of me for the entire process. So, I continued writing on my own with no direction.

I wanted the book to be about 220 pages, but my progress was very slow. Over the years, I got most of the book done and decided I needed help getting the story out to people. I started pursuing publishers, or someone who could take my idea to the next level. I tried contacting a few people and companies but everything seemed to fall to the wayside.

God began pushing me again to finish the book, to bring it to completion. I would work on it for a week or two and then it would take a back seat to my other priorities. Then, finally one day, God moved me to approach another man in my church named Rusty. Rusty agreed to follow behind me, clean up my grammar and make suggestions.

He was willing to read the first chapter and show me my grammatical mistakes. When I received the first chapter back from him, it was covered with red ink and with lots of changes in sentence structure. He also said I was missing something called descriptive writing. (That's how much I know about writing; don't even ask me what a verb, adjective or a compound sentence is.) When I asked what descriptive writing was, he gave me a few examples and suggested I read a few books that showed what it looks like. One book was *"Piercing the Darkness"* by Frank Peretti, which I had read years ago.

After I learned what descriptive writing was, I started rewriting my book. I finished chapter one and two, and then I got irritated because I just wanted it to be done. At the same time, I was listening to *The Pilgrim's Progress* by John Bunyan on CD. As I was listening to it, I noticed it was mostly dialog and not descriptive writing, so I decided I must have gotten sidetracked with Rusty's direction. I decided to call my pastor on the way to work and discuss how I thought I had been sidetracked by Rusty's suggestions. He let me ramble for a while, and finally I made it to work. The conversation had been one-sided, my side.

A funny thing happened after that conversation. Four

hours after I got to work, I noticed my brother Brian was sitting in the lunchroom. I decided to ask him if he wanted to read chapter one because he had not read any of it since I had written the beginning pages.

He read the first chapter, came over to me and said, "This is awesome; it was like I was there." I immediately gave him chapter two and three, and he came over to me after he read them. I asked what he thought. He said, 'Chapter one and two were great, but chapter three is missing something. It could be me because I need to get back to work, but it seems it was missing descriptive writing."

I could not believe it. There were those words again, "Descriptive Writing". He had used those exact words. At that point I laughed and said, "Okay, Okay Lord, I will continue." With renewed passion, I got the book three-quarters of the way finished when the wind in my sails died.

Then, God gave me another push to complete the book during a men's retreat at Camp Spofford, which is in New Hampshire. There, at the men's retreat, during a break I showed the first couple of chapters to a fellow brother named Andreas. He said the book was good and asked how much was left till it was completed. I said, "The Lord is pushing me to finish it, but I keep dying. It is hard to stay motivated."

His reply is what helped me to finish the book. He said, "If God told you to write a book and if He is telling you to finish it now, you have a choice. You can make time and get it done, or He can allow your leg to break then you will have plenty of time to get it done."

After hearing that, I decided I needed to finish the book quickly, because, if I can, I prefer to avoid pain. I would rather follow the Lord with Him whispering to me saying, "Go that way" than be brought to the woodshed in order for Him to get my attention.

After that conversation, I found a publisher and finished the book within two months.

In closing, this also came across my path when there was no wind in my sails, [1]Beyond Imagination:

[It has not] entered into the heart of man the things which God has prepared for those who love Him. — 1 Corinthians 2:9

A college professor at a Christian school perceived that his students held a distorted view of heaven; they considered it to be static and boring. So, to stir their imaginations, he asked them these questions:

"Do you wish you would wake up tomorrow morning to discover that the person you loved most passionately loved you even more? Wake up hearing music you have always loved but had never heard with such infinite joy before? Rise to the new day as if you were just discovering the Pacific Ocean? Wake up without feeling guilty about anything at all? See to the very core of yourself, and like everything you see? Wake up breathing God as if He were air? Loving to love Him? And loving everybody else in the bargain?"

In response to that professor's intriguing questions, the students all lifted their hands. If that's what heaven will be like and even infinitely more so, they certainly wanted to be there.

"I go to prepare a place for you," Jesus told His disciples (John 14:2). We all share the desire — really a deep-down yearning — to be in that glorious home forever. It is a place of indescribable bliss. And the supreme blessing will be the presence of our Lord Jesus Christ Himself!

— Vernon Grounds

When we all get to heaven, what a day of rejoicing that will be! When we all see Jesus, we'll sing and shout the victory. — *Hewitt*

---

[1]Our Daily Bread, November 21, 2009

Chapter 1: Streets of Gold

I T was a beautiful crisp day with light blue skies hanging over the kingdom like a canopy. The wind blew above and caused large white clouds to tumble, roll and change shape as they broke apart. It was a picturesque scene in the heavens above. It was so beautiful that it made Jonathan Stone think of a master painter's canvas portraying the image of the perfect day with clouds advancing into the sunset. The temperature was perfect, not too hot and not too cold. It was the type of day that could put a smile on any face. The weather was absolutely flawless, yet everyday was ideal for the entire time Jonathan Stone lived in this awesome kingdom.

As he walked down the street, the wind carried the fragrance of flowers. Occasionally, a hint of fresh cut grass drifted through the air, almost like the smell of spring. Jonathan felt the soft breeze fall upon his face as it continued its path through his hair, then into the distance. He drank in the beauty and the fragrances that were all around him.

"How long have I been here?" he asked himself. "Has it been ten, twenty or perhaps fifty years, maybe more?"

He laughed quietly and a slight smile crossed his face. "It's hard to keep track of time in eternity."

As he walked along the Kingdom's streets of pure gold, his eyes looked down and admired the patterns that the bricks made as they crisscrossed each other. Some bricks were deep gold in color, while others had a much softer tint that caused the patterns to jump out. The city's Main Street was massive in width, like the Mississippi River flowing down through St. Louis. The street also rolled to the left and bent to the right as it continued on endlessly into the horizon. As he walked, he noticed how many of the other streets joined into the main street, and yet the patterns the bricks made were never broken. It reminded him of puzzle pieces fitting perfectly together.

Walking was one of his daily routines. He has always enjoyed the beauty of the kingdom, and he truly loved exploring the depths of the kingdom that seemed to expand endlessly in all directions. A deep sigh of contentment flowed from his mouth and a smile brightened even more of his face. He was thinking about how happy he was, how content and at peace. A deep satisfying joy began to fill him as he reflected on these things.

Jonathan walked for miles and miles, never once growing tired or weary. His eyes were captivated by everything around him, from the sky above to the streets below. On the left of him were thousands upon thousands of gorgeous houses and buildings of every color imaginable. The houses varied from one to another in amazing proportions, yet each one shined forth in its own uniqueness, beauty and splendor, never once robbing, but always complementing its neighboring house. On the right of him flowed the greatest river in the kingdom.

As Jonathan was walking, the street bent to the right ahead of him and a house caught his attention. It was not small or large, but moderate in size. It seemed to shine and sparkle and stand out among the other houses. As he got closer, he noticed that the outside walls of the house were decorated with millions of different colored gems. There were diamonds, rubies, sapphires and other precious jewels. They sparkled and danced on the walls as the light of the city hit them. His eyes were mesmerized by the colors, which no human eye had ever seen or imagined, reflecting off this one home in particular.

Finally, he reached the house and stopped to look at it in greater detail. Walking forward he noticed a carved image above the door. It was a desert scene of an oasis, carved in great detail; even the blades of the grass could be made out among the palm trees, flowers and bushes that surround a desert pool. On the side of the door were inlays of pure gold showing similar images that captured the eye's attention. He reached out and let his hand slide gently over the inlays and found it to be as smooth as glass. As he stepped back, something hit the back of his leg. Turning, he saw it was a decorated bench. He noticed that the back of the bench had the same carvings and inlays as the house in front of him. He decided to sit down, relax and drink in the beauty of the day.

Jonathan let out a long slow breath and said silently, "This place is so awesome! I still can't believe that I'm here walking down these streets."

A hint of excitement fell upon his face as he looked to his left, and then right. He thought to himself, "There are so many places yet to see and explore. I could walk for the next ten thousand years and see but a small piece, a mere portion of this massive kingdom."

His thoughts turned back to the days of his old life, and that old world in which he used to live so long ago. Images of his past life began to flood his mind. He remembered the street he grew up on as a child and the house in which he lived. It was a brown three-family house with yellow trim. There were two small apartments downstairs and a larger three-bedroom apartment upstairs. He remembered the wood paneling in the living room, the square yellow and blue tiles in the kitchen and an enclosed porch looking down on the trees and street below. His house was one of many two and three family homes in the neighborhood.

His memory brought him to a river. It was the Connecticut River; he remembered it snaking its way downstream to a bridge, then over a dam and continued on until it reached the Atlantic Ocean. He also remembered the mountain that overlooked the river. He smiled and said to himself, "Mount Tom."

He could still remember so many places, faces and even conversations he had. But it was all gone now, ancient history. The memories of his past life were still fresh and they probably always would be. His memories reminded him of a dream, of some distant land in another day and another time that was once lived a very, very long time ago.

Jonathan recalled how that old world disappeared; it vanished and was no more. It was on a day that no one expected, just another ordinary day. [1]People were laughing, eating, drinking, and just living their lives when the end came upon everyone unexpectedly. God had come back, and every eye had seen Him.

Jonathan remembered the events of that day, and of the days that followed. He recalled when the [2]sky began to roll back like

---

[1] Luke 17:26-30
[2] Revelation 1:14

a scroll, as if the universe was a map being rolled up to be put away. He watched in amazement as every mountain and island was removed from its place, like a blanket being stretched out and the ripples disappearing.

He remembered watching the [3]heavens, all the stars and planets, being destroyed by an all-consuming fire. He watched as everything seemed to melt away from the intense heat. It reminded him of lead being melted in a furnace. Jonathan remembered watching this spectacular scene unfold before him from heaven.

He had the perfect vantage point, and all the people of the kingdom watched with him, everyone was filled with great joy and excitement. He had heard that this event could not be matched in all of history except for one other time. The days when the [4]angels sang for joy when God created the first heavens and earth by his creative power. This last event was different though, because this time, all the saints were present with the angels, and they sang together with joy when they watched the [5]old order of things pass away and the new come forward; a new creation was revealed.

As he was thinking of these things, the King of Kings and Lord of Lords appeared before him. Jonathan was not startled or afraid by this sudden appearance, but instead, a great excitement began to emerge within him.

---

[3] 1 Peter 3:10
[4] Job 38:7
[5] 2 Corinthians 5:17

Chapter 2: Walking with the King

The Lord was dressed in a white robe that flowed down to His feet; a golden sash was wrapped around His chest. Jonathan noticed that the sash was woven from pure gold with threads of blue, purple and scarlet yarn woven in. ⁶The Lord's head and hair were white like snow, and His eyes were like blazing fire. His feet were like bronze glowing in a furnace. Jonathan knew that the whiteness represented the King's holiness and His eyes, ablaze, represented how He could chase away the evil that claims a man's heart, breaking the binding chains of sin that hold him fast. (As the years went by Jonathan would grasp an even greater and deeper insight into these attributes of the Lord as they were revealed to him.)

At once, Jonathan stood up and bowed low before Him. The Lord walked to his side, turned and sat down. He gestured for Jonathan to sit beside Him as He tapped the seat.

The Lord looked at Jonathan and said, "This home is indeed beautiful." He asked with a smile, "Do you know who lives here?"

"No, I don't," Jonathan replied with an inquisitive look upon his face.

Looking at the house, Jesus said, "This, indeed, is one of the most beautiful homes in the entire kingdom; yet this person was not well known on earth. Many people never even considered him and oftentimes looked right past him, but my light shined brightly through him to his generation. What the world overlooks and despises becomes a precious jewel in the heavenly kingdom. For what the world lifted up has come crashing down and what it looked down upon has been exalted." Very excitedly Jonathan asked, "Lord, who is it? Who lives here?" Jesus said with a grin, "As an old song goes, 'if you want to be great in God's kingdom, you must become the servant of all.'" Jonathan asked again with even more excitement, "Lord, who is it?"

Jesus smiled and said with a little laugh, "You will see him soon enough." He then stood up and turned to Jonathan saying,

"Let's take a walk."

Jonathan stood up, and the Lord put His hand on his shoulder and said, "Let's walk toward [6]my throne, where the River of Life begins."

They began to walk together down the streets of gold in the heavenly kingdom.

"My beloved Jonathan, did you know that your earthly life was very dear to me? Did you know you have always been precious in my sight? Let me show you your life from the very beginning. You will see that in [7]all things I worked together for your good and the good of those who loved me. I was there at your side and I walked with you all the days of your life!"

Then the Lord opened up Jonathan's mind and began showing him his early years.

Jonathan watched in amazement as a mist of smoke appeared out of thin air. As images began to take shape before him, he felt he could almost reach out and touch the past. He noticed that it was early summer, the sun was rising and the dew on the grass was sparkling from its rays. He could even smell the grass and feel the heat of the sun as it chased away the coolness of the morning.

As the Lord made one scene unfold into another, he found himself looking into a hospital room and recognized his mother, Amy Stone, in labor. He even heard her cry out as a contraction came. His ears perked up as he heard his father try to comfort her. Jonathan watched as his father said with a grin, "Come on Amy, is it really all that bad?"

Jonathan shook his head and laughed, "Dad always tried to make a joke out of everything." Jonathan also noticed that the joke did not go over all too well.

He watched as the contractions and pain finally stopped, and in amazement, he saw himself being born. He saw the excitement on their faces. He listened as a nurse asked what the baby's name was, and his parents responded with the name of Jonathan, Jonathan Stone.

---

[6] Revelation 22:1
[7] Romans 8:28

As Jonathan watched the scenes of his life unfold, he soon discovered that he was [8]born into a family that suited him perfectly. He now understood that his family was made especially for him. He saw how the Lord worked behind the scenes and moved in the circumstances of his life and the lives of the ones he loved.

He saw how He molded each of them into the men and women they were to become.

Jonathan watched how the Lord kept him from harm's way and delivered him from the situations that would have destroyed his life otherwise.

As they walked, Jonathan turned to the Lord and asked Him, "If I knew back then how much you were involved in my life, would I have lived differently?"

Jesus smiled and said, [9]"The Spirit is always willing, but the flesh is very weak. Truth and knowledge can indeed set you free. When truth is revealed and understanding dawns on the heart, the man of God will have a desire to walk in the path of the righteous. His heart's desire is to follow that path in truth and understanding."

Jonathan said with a little frustration, "It seemed that I knew the truth, but I didn't have enough strength to follow it."

Jesus gave an understanding smile and said, [10]"There were many enemies on that path that wanted to steal what was sown. The devil was one of those enemies that crouched along the way; he was like a roaring lion who always tried to put fear and doubts in the hearts of believers, making that path seem impossible to follow.

"He would often whisper in their ears saying, 'God did not really speak to you; it was your own mind telling you these things. You are already on the right path and everything is going well. Don't doubt or change anything because if God was really calling you, the path would be much easier and clearer to follow.'

"The devil would also try to bring discouragement to those who stepped forward in faith. He would say, 'That way is much too hard for you and you do not have the strength to walk in that

---

[8] Acts 18:26-28
[9] Matthew 26:41
[10] Matthew 13:19-22

direction. Go ahead, try to walk that way, but remember the past; you always failed then and you are sure to fail now.'

"He would sow seeds of despair all along the paths of one's life. Many times, he whispered in the ears of the faithful and said, 'The Lord is not with you; He has forsaken you. Examine yourself and you will see. Can you feel His presence in you? You know you cannot. He has abandoned you and left you because you have failed Him so many times.

Think about it, maybe you never really came to Him in faith. You are still probably in your sins and are separated from His love.'

"Doubt and fear would then enter into the heart, and oftentimes rob what was sown."

Jonathan said with a shudder, "I have been there so many times. I felt I was not in the sheep pen and had wandered away from your presence. Many times, I would question if I really was one of yours. Sometimes I questioned myself by wondering if I really had faith, and if I sincerely came to you for salvation at all."

As they walked, Jesus stopped and turned to Jonathan. He put a loving hand on his shoulder and said in gentle words, "My Spirit continually fought with your flesh. He would call you, and woo you by whispering my loving words into your heart. Over and over again He would direct you to your favorite verse which says, [11]'Anyone who comes to me, I will never drive away.'

"You would often question your faith by saying, 'I wonder if my faith is real. Am I lying to myself? Have I deceived myself? Maybe I didn't come fully and sincerely to Him. Maybe I'm not really one of His chosen people after all?'"

"Those first steps are the hardest and most difficult ones in the path of life. My Spirit continually worked to remove the doubt from your heart and made your salvation secure, as if it were built on a solid rock that could not be shaken."

With a dawning look, Jonathan replied, "I remember

---

[11] John 6:37

fighting those thoughts and feelings and finally saying to myself, 'Can I really come to Him perfectly, with my whole heart?' Then I learned the truth... I can only come with the heart I have and the doubts I carry. I can't clean up my act and present myself any better. I have to come as I am, with empty hands and trust in your promises that you would never drive me away."

Jesus replied, "Even in the sheep pen, one can see and feel a storm coming. One may feel a blast of wind, while another may feel the cold rain pouring down. Yet another sees the lightning striking all around him, while others hear the thunder and their hearts begin to tremble. The storms in that old life were sure to come."

"One day, my Spirit spoke this truth into your heart, 'the storms of life flow over the sheep pen too. Just because there is a storm raging, does not mean you have wandered away from the fold.'"

Jonathan smiled in remembrance and said, "I remember how the truth became a great comfort to my soul; the truth shined like a bright light on the dark seas. I shared it with many people whose hearts were, like mine, shaken by the storms of life."

With a knowing smile, Jesus said, "You were indeed a comfort to the broken hearted, as I moved you to share what you learned. I know those were hard trials for you to go through, but I wanted to produce in you a heart of a shepherd, someone who would not muddy the waters where my sheep drink."

Jonathan laughed and added, "I have certainly failed many times as a shepherd." Jesus responded with a smile, "I know... but not completely."

They began walking again on the streets of gold beside the banks of the [12]River of Life that continued on into the horizon. The river was very wide, and a faint outline of buildings and houses could be seen on the other side. The water had a light blue tint, yet it was crystal clear. One could see the riverbed covered with smooth worn stones that created shadows as the light hit them. Various forms of life could be seen darting this way and that from

---

[12] Revelation 22:1

one rock to another. The pleasing sound of the water could be heard as it splashed along the shore and gently rolled over rocks that tried to hinder the river's endless progress.

Jonathan's eyes and ears could never seem to get their fill of the River of Life. It was like seeing it new every day.

"This River is so beautiful; I'm really looking forward to exploring it to its very end."

Jesus laughed and said, "How do you know it ends?"

Jonathan was about to respond when he heard someone sitting on a bench they had just passed, singing a familiar song, "If you want to be great in God's kingdom, learn to be the servant of all."

Jonathan turned his head quickly in the direction of the song. There was a man there that he did not recognize. He was about to speak when Jesus said, with a big smile. "Yes, that's the man who lives in the house you were admiring. Remember? I said, 'You will see him soon enough.'"

Jonathan was about to turn to meet the man, but the Lord, smiling, urged him forward. "Let's continue on with our walk."

"Jonathan, I want you to see how much I was involved in your birth, I want you to grow more and more in your understanding and [13]grasp how wide, how long, how high and how deep my love is for you and for all my people."

The Lord began to pour out His words into Jonathan's mind and heart giving him more truths to dwell upon. Jonathan felt a greater and deeper love for his Lord, if that were even possible."

Their walk ended at the Throne and Jesus said, "I enjoyed our walk, and I would like you to share what you learned with a very special person. He is waiting for you at your home."

Jonathan said appreciatively, "Lord, thank you for always being with me and walking with me in a very special way. I praise you that I am yours, and that I have all of eternity to be with you, to learn from you and to enjoy you. It's so easy here to give my whole heart to you."

Jesus said, "I love you too, Jonathan, and I enjoy our time

---

[13] Ephesians 3:18

spent together. Remember, you have all of eternity to enjoy me and learn more of me. This will never be taken away from you. Now go, you have a special guest waiting for you. He will make your heart leap."

Jonathan headed toward home with great wonder and anticipation.

Chapter 3: The Long-Lost Friend

J onathan headed towards home. As he walked, he passed thousands upon thousands of men and women from every generation. Some walked two by two, while others gathered in groups of five or ten, fifty and even hundreds. Some were working, some were playing, but all were enjoying the beauty of the kingdom, the great inheritance they had received.

All the way home, Jonathan wondered who this special guest might be. After walking many, many miles, he turned the corner and his house came within view. There, sitting on the steps of his house, was a man dressed in a white robe. Jonathan could not make out the man's features from afar, but as he came closer, he noticed that there was something familiar about him. The man turned and noticed Jonathan walking toward him. He stood up and walked towards Jonathan. As the gap between them closed, each could tell from the other's expression that they were trying to figure out who the other was. Finally, recognition began to dawn on both of them simultaneously.

"Jonathan," The man said with an excited voice.

"Chuck, is that you? Is it really you?" Jonathan responded in disbelief.

Finally, confirmation set in and both their hearts seemed to dance with joy. As they reached each other, Jonathan's memories shot back to the old world where they had been great friends, but circumstances had separated them. Flashes of their times together sprang from deep within him. Scenes of fishing on the Connecticut River, camping in Burlington, VT, Bible studies and family gatherings filled his mind. Jonathan felt a lump forming in his throat and his eyes were becoming moist with tears of joy. Just seeing Chuck brought great excitement to his heart, and each could tell that the other felt the same way.

"The Lord said, "Jonathan, you have a very special visitor that will make your heart leap." He was right. Just knowing that you are here and that our friendship is just beginning again brings great joy to my heart."

"I was very excited when the Lord said that He had someone special for me to meet. I was wondering who it might be. As I was walking here, I thought maybe the house would give some hint of who lived there. No hint was given and I only began to recognize you when we were face to face. When I finally knew that it was you, my heart rejoiced. Jonathan, you were a very, very dear friend to me. I have always treasured the memories we had together."

Jonathan nodded his head in agreement and said, "We had many great times together in that old world. We used to talk about growing old together and enjoying each other's company. Those were our plans, but the Lord had better plans."

"I remember when we started to drift apart. I moved to another town and a different church, while you moved to another state. You settled in Pennsylvania and I stayed in Massachusetts. The gap of a few hundred miles between us seemed more like a world apart."

Chuck shook his head and said quietly, "That old world separated me from many of the people I loved. I'm sure many of our brothers and sisters felt a similar pain in their separation from their loved ones. Separation can be heart wrenching; people move away, as in our case, but the worst separation was the deaths of the ones we loved. That was a very, very sad world we once lived in; with much pain to bear and sorrow to drink."

Jonathan replied, "I have also seen something interesting in these times of separation. Our Lord always comforted us in our sorrows, oftentimes by bringing other people into our lives. What He takes away, He often gives back, and as He closes one door, He opens another. Many people came in and out of my life and I developed a love for many of them. I see now that God has used these times to spread his love throughout the church and into a fallen world. We were like seeds that were scattered, but much grain can be produced. Wherever the church was scattered, Christ's love spread out to the multitudes."

Chuck agreed wholeheartedly and said, "You're right. God had something much better in mind than what we could have ever planned. He took our little idea of growing old together and made it into a grand plan. We don't just have each other; we have a great multitude of loved ones that followed us right into the kingdom. We're not limited to a few years, but instead, we can enjoy each other's company for eternity."

"Here, distance doesn't matter; my home is in the northern most part of the kingdom, twelve hundred miles away from here by man's old measurements. The distance between us is now like a walk in the park."

Jonathan laughed and said, "You know I have always been a talker; I can go on and on. I didn't even think of inviting you in. Come on in and see what the Lord has done for me. We can sit down and continue our conversation inside."

So, Jonathan and Chuck walked up the stairs, stepped across a threshold, opened the door and stepped into an eternal home.

As Chuck stepped in, he noticed that the first room was rectangular in shape and large enough to hold forty to fifty people comfortably. He looked to his left and saw six large arched windows overlooking the large cobblestone path that followed alongside the River of Life. His eyes caught the light as it reflected off the river and seemed to dance as it went through the windows. It colored the living room with shards of moving light. A warm gentle breeze blew past him and carried with it the sweet smell of flowers; lilacs he thought. He continued to watch as the wind blew across the river, over the bushes, through the trees and into the room. The smell of the flowers and the warm air continued to flow gently past him. Chuck then took in a deep breath; slowly and effortlessly he breathed out a long sigh of contentment.

To the right was a large table with twelve chairs placed neatly around it. The table had two large woven baskets filled with various colored fruit, vegetables and flowers that seemed to overflow onto the table. The left side of the room had two large tan arched couches facing each other with a huge oval glass table in the middle. On each end of the sitting area were two large cushioned chairs with plenty of space for people to maneuver through. The walls of the rooms had a light blue tint. The floor was made out of some heavenly exotic wood and the grain swirled its way throughout the room. In one section large colored stones were inlayed into the wood forming a rectangular pattern marking off a sitting area.

"Wow, the Lord knows how to build a home. What a beautiful place He has given you. It suits you, and I imagine it fits all the spiritual gifts that you have in your service to the King."

Jonathan said, "He certainly made all our homes fit who we are and the ministries in which we serve. As you can see, my ministry is fellowship. I have so many opportunities to serve our Lord by serving the heirs of the kingdom who enter in." "So, who else lives here? Chuck asked.

"My earthly wife, my family and all those I love and cherish in Christ are here, or very close by. I am so glad that what God has joined together, He has not separated. As you know we are not married or given in marriage, but the Lord certainly did not separate us from the ones we loved. He did something far better, even beyond what our earthly minds would have or could have ever imagined or understood."

Chuck smiled in agreement and replied, "I have been welcomed into so many homes from every generation and culture. It is amazing how He has joined the entire heavenly kingdom together. We are all like different pieces of a wall, interlocking together, built on a great foundation that has been raised up to become the heavenly kingdom."

"I notice how all of our homes reflect our individual ministries and even reflect who we are. It is awesome how our individual personalities, our gift and talents, were carried into eternity and into our new heavenly homes."

"I am so glad He left the sin behind." Jonathan added while shaking his head.

Jonathan turned and looked straight at Chuck. Grinning, he said, "Guess what? I have a surprise for you. I was walking with the Lord a little while ago and He blessed me by pouring out His words into my heart. He asked me to share them with you."

"What did He say?"

"We talked about many things, but He asked me to tell you how He was involved in my early life, behind the scenes. He told me to share this with you. Grab a seat, and I'll begin."

They both walked into the living room and sat down; Chuck stretched out and waited for Jonathan to start the conversation.

"The Lord said He wanted to show me how much He was involved in my life, even from birth. He wanted me to understand [14]how wide, long, high and deep His love is for me and for all His people."

Chuck added, "The Lord has already shared so many things with me, personally. He also used many saints and angels to share His blessing and to minister His grace to me in its various forms. I have truly been blessed beyond measure."

Jonathan began, "The Lord told me that He made the very first man, Adam. He then said that [15]He made all mankind and every nation so that man would fill the whole world. He then determined the times, dates and years set for them, and even the exact places where they should live. He said He did this so that men would seek Him, perhaps reach out for Him and find Him, though He mentioned He was never far from each one of us.

He looked directly into my eyes, put His right hand upon

---

[14] Ephesians 3:18
[15] Acts 17:26-28

my shoulder and said, 'Jonathan, [16]I have chosen you before the creation of the world to be holy and blameless in my sight. In my great love, I have chosen you and adopted you to be my beloved son. I did this for my own good pleasure and will. I, and I alone, did all this.

I [17]knitted you together in your mother's womb and I created your innermost being. I have loved you with an everlasting love, and [18]I have always drawn you with my cords of loving-kindness. For you were mine from the very beginning and now I am yours for all of eternity.'

"Chuck, to hear those words come from His mouth, it made my heart faint within me and my soul seemed to burst with emotions."

"Oh, I wish I was there! He has said similar things to me, and I am sure He has said the same to all His beloved. You know what I hate? Those same wonderful words were made known to me in the old world, yet they did not affect me like they do here. I heard those same words written in His book and oftentimes they fell on deaf ears. I knew and believed these truths, but my heart seemed grounded, I could not fly. It was as if my wings were clipped so that I could not soar on the heights."

Jonathan got up and said, "Let's go sit by the river and I'll finish telling you everything He said." They both got up, and as the door was closing Jonathan said, "Do you think I should lock it?"

They laughed together as they headed down the stairs, across the street and into the park that followed the river. They followed a cobblestone path that gradually wound its way up a small hill. Upon reaching the summit, they found a spot overlooking the River of Life. They both sat down on the grass, which was soft to the touch and had the smell of being freshly cut.

They sat, enjoying the sound of the river and admiring the trees that scattered the landscape. In the far distance, a huge mountain range could be seen; it was known as Emmanuel's Range.

---

[16] Ephesians 1:4-5
[17] Psalm 139:13
[18] Jeremiah 31:3

As they looked across the river, they could see the outline of fruit trees with their branches bending to the ground because of the vast amount of fruit growing on them. They had a bird's eye view of the park and the city that stretched out in every direction as far as the eye could see.

They looked down and watched hundreds of saints, angels and cherubim enjoying each other's company. Some walked together on the cobblestone paths below, others gathered under trees in the park, and some were walking down the streets of gold. They sat for a little while watching the river flow into the distance toward Emmanuel's mountains.

They were enjoying the bounty they received, [19]their inheritance that was kept in heaven for them; the inheritance that could never perish, spoil or fade.

Jonathan was about to continue with his story when he heard footsteps behind him. As they turned, they saw their Heavenly Father approaching them in the cool of the day.

---

[19] 1 Peter 1:4

Chapter 4: Father, Son, and Holy Spirit

A s they saw Him, they stood up and then bowed low to the ground. When they raised their heads, a brilliant light encompassed the Father and the glory of His presence burst forth. They tried to shield their eyes from the light, but it still seemed to penetrate their innermost being. They heard the Lord's voice and as they slowly opened their eyes, they saw the Lord Jesus coming out of the light, shining forth like the sun in all its brilliance. Around him swirled a great and powerful wind mixed with fire. The two men could feel the wind and the heat upon their faces. They watched in awe as the wind swirled and the fire blazed around the Father, Son and Holy Spirit.

Jonathan and Chuck just stood there, speechless, overcome by the spectacular scene. They were about to fall down and worship when their heavenly Father said to them, "Jonathan and Chuck, I love you with an everlasting love. You are very precious to me and honored in my sight; you are my beloved children. [20]It is truly my joy to give you the Kingdom." His voice was soft and tender, like the sound of a groom saying to his bride, "I will always love you."

"We have come to share with you the mysteries of your earthy lives and to answer your present questions. We delight in explaining to our beloved children how we have always worked together in your earthly lives, [21]for I am the one who has chosen you according to my foreknowledge. You have been sanctified by the work of the Holy Spirit and you were called to obedience to Jesus Christ and to be covered by His precious blood that was poured out for you on Calvary."

When the Father smiled at them, they could actually see and feel the love and the joy flowing from the light of His presence.

"My sons, you wonder why you didn't respond to all our love and goodness that was given to you in your earthly life? You

---

[20] Luke 12:32

[21] I Peter 1:2

wonder why our words that you hear today, [22]words that are living, active and sharper than any two edge sword, didn't seem to penetrate the very depths of your soul in the old world?

"Many of the same words you hear today were written down for your encouragement in the old world. They were always yours for the taking. My heart's desire was that you would have [23]tasted and seen all the good things; things that were already yours, that came from our hands. Many times, you tasted and saw those blessings and you were never disappointed. For centuries my people read the Scriptures and dwelt on these same precious promises which comforted them in their sorrow. I used the words of the Scriptures to capture and [24]awaken love in the hearts of my children.

[25] "The problem is that sin was present, and oftentimes robbed what was sown. The worries of that old life choked out the words of love and hindered the blessings that grew from them. Here, sin is removed and our love can be fully experienced. We prepared this place for you because we wanted your love to reach maturity. Only then could you taste and see all the love we have for you, an endless supply that will always make your joy complete."

At this point, Jesus stepped forward and reached out and placed His hands on each of their shoulders. As His hands were upon them, the folds of his robe slid back and they could see the deep wounds and scars that had redeemed them from their past life of sin and death.

Nothing more needed to be said, their hearts were captured and nothing could hinder them or stand in their way of seeing, enjoying, loving and worshipping the Lords of the Kingdom. They understood more, and they realized to an even greater extent, that this was what their lives were truly made for; they were created to be in the presence of the living God.

The Holy Spirit began impressing upon them to [28]drink deeply from the wells of salvation; to fully grasp and receive the

---

[22] Hebrews 4:12
[23] Psalm 34:8
[24] Song of Solomon 3:5
[25] Matthew 13:19

words that were spoken to them. The Spirit took the words of the Father and   Son and poured them over the two men. It reminded Jonathan of a great waterfall in the springtime, pouring forth and flooding the valley below. They both stood there speechless, beside the River of Life, among those great [26]trees that grow beside the river that brings healing to the nations.

Just as quick as it happened, they found themselves alone with Jesus, but they were not really alone for the Father, Son and Holy Spirit always dwell in and fill the entire kingdom with their presence.

Jesus said to Jonathan, "You have so many other questions you want to ask me, but I know you want to ask them only because you want our conversations to continue and   never   end. I   say   to you [27]"Ask and it will be given to you; seek and you will find; knock and the door will be opened to you. For everyone who asks, receives; he who seeks, finds; and to him who knocks, the door will be opened."

Jonathan knew he had plenty of time, all of eternity, actually, in which to ask his many questions. He knew they would be answered at the appropriate time, for the Lord now dwells among His people. His real desires and pleasures were just being with the Lord, to be at his side and to feel his wonderful presence surrounding him.

Jesus continued, "Many times you have wondered why I seemed to wait so long to answer my promises. I know you understand many of these things, but I want to peel back more of these hidden layers of truth so that you can better understand the depths of my promises.

"You have heard many stories of faithful saints praying for their loved ones, some never even seeing them come to faith because death separated them, while many others have prayed for decades for loved ones and finally, they are saved, but so many years later. You are wondering why I held back or delayed my salvation,

---

[26] Revelation 22:2
[27] Matthew 7:7

when I could have revealed myself and saved them in a moment, in the blink of an eye?

"Many of your brothers and sisters asked similar questions here and in the old world. You are asking what many have debated and tried to reconcile since the time of Adam and the ancient patriarchs. Many have searched the Scriptures for answers to where my loving kindness, desire and will intersect with human responsibility. Very few people in that old world understood the depths of the human heart and how it can be held captive by the chains of sin. They also didn't have a full understanding of my desire to save; the power of my love to overcome all obstacles and to move all things according to my good pleasure, desire and will.

"Yes, it's true. I can save a soul as quickly as a man can blink an eye. I can make the human heart willing to believe on me in an instant. I have created every heart, so I know every heart and what it desires. [28]I know what is in a man."

With a smile, Jesus said, "What is better, to save a soul instantly or save a soul at the right time, so that it will bring more glory and more praise to your heavenly Father's name?"

Then the Lord explained to Jonathan and Chuck how God's sovereignty and human responsibility intersected, they knew now what so many debated throughout the ages.

Jonathan said to the Lord, "I always knew in the old world that your ways were just, even though at times I couldn't reconcile them. Sadly, many times in the old world I was [32]tossed back and forth like a wave of the sea, by various passages in Scripture, as well as the thoughts that entered my mind and the challenges of life."

Jesus said, "You are not alone in your thinking. All of my people have, at one time or another, been tossed back and forth by life's many challenges. Many found comfort when they trusted me with their future. Many have learned to lean on this particular truth in difficult times, [29]'The secret things are for God, and the revealed things are for us.' Many people lived and walked by faith in that

---

[28] John 2:23-25
[29] Deuteronomy 29:29

promise, when life's trials blinded them and hindered their progress. They found great comfort in knowing that nothing happens without my knowledge, nor is anything ever out of my control."

They knew my ears were attentive to their call, my eyes never left them, and my arms were ready to catch them, carry them and sustain them if they were to fall. They knew that I would never leave them or forsake them; I would never leave their side."

Jonathan said, "Lord, I love spending these special times with you. My heart and soul always seem to sing for joy in the kingdom, but even more so when you are near. All the difficulties of that old life have long since been washed away by your presence and the seas of those earthly difficulties have been settled long ago by your comforting hands. You always put a new song within my heart."

Jesus said, "You both have a lot of questions, and there is even more that you have not even considered. We will take many walks together and sit by the River of Life. It is my delight to open your hearts to all of life's mysteries, for that earthly veil has been removed and the hidden things will continue to be made known."

Chuck felt the same as Jonathan did and felt a deep desire welling up from his heart to somehow show his appreciation to his Lord, some tangible way to bless Him, some way to demonstrate his love for Him.

As they sat at the Lord's side, he said in a voice filled with emotion.

"Lord, I love being here with you, to be able to walk with you and to hear your voice. Whenever you are near, my very heart overflows and the very depths of my soul are satisfied. All the difficulties of that old life have disappeared like a mist, and all those ocean waves that have tossed me back and forth have settled. My life is now surrounded in the harbor of your love. It is such a wonderful feeling knowing that my life can never be buffeted by those earthly waves again."

Jonathan added, "Lord, I find it amazing that you can be with each one of us in a special way, and that you can share yourself completely."

Jonathan remembered the Master's word that said,

[30]"He fills the universe" and [31]"where can we flee from His presence?"

As they stood beside the River of Life, many other saints started walking up the cobblestone path to the top of the hill, which is called Shepherd's Hill.

First one came, and then two, then ten, twenty and the little group continued to grow until a vast crowd had gathered with them beside the river.

Somewhere in the crowd, the sound of singing started, then more and more saints joined in. The song they began singing was an old song, from the old world, but it had been changed anew in the kingdom.

[32] "O soul, never weary or troubled, always in His light, never darkness to see. There is always love, behold our Savior, so abundant and free!

Turn your eyes upon Jesus; look full into His wonderful face; those things of earth have grown strangely dim, in the light of His glory and grace."

---

[30] Ephesians 4:10
[31] Psalm 139:7
[32] Hymn: Turn your eyes upon Jesus, written by Helen Lemmel

Chapter 5: The Great Assembly

One day Jonathan's work brought him to the northern part of the kingdom. After his duties were completed, he decided to surprise Chuck with a visit.

As Jonathan was making his way there, he passed many homes where he could hear joyful music flowing out of the windows and doors that were open. While at other houses, he could hear people talking, laughing and just enjoying each other's company. The city was always filled with life, and the heirs of the kingdom lived there and enjoyed it to the fullest.

Jonathan thought to himself, "Only God could create a city filled with so much life, joy and peace."

He finally arrived at Chuck's house and knocked on the door. As the door opened, a smile came upon Chuck's face as he said, "Hey brother, come on in."

As Jonathan entered, he scanned the room to see how the Lord blessed him in his eternal home. As he looked around the room, he noticed all the books that filled every nook and cranny. To his left were three very large bookcases with chairs, couches and end tables between them; Jonathan thought that there must be thousands upon thousands of books on those shelves.

"Check this out," Chuck said. "I have Bibles from every generation, culture and language."

Jonathan walked over and looked at the books; every inch of the bookcase was filled from top to bottom. He recognized some of the titles, such as *The Pilgrim's Progress, Foxe's Book of Martyrs, Hind's Feet On High Places*, hymnals and other literature from every century and culture. Many of the books he knew were not from the Old World but had been written there by other saints in the kingdom.

"Wow, this is quite a collection! You always enjoyed reading and writing, and it looks like that joy followed you right here into the kingdom."

"Indeed, I love reading and writing and trying to uncover

the mysteries of our God. You know the saying, [33]"it is the glory of God to conceal a matter; to search out what is hidden is man's desire.' I find it fun and exciting. It has given me great joy when the Lord tells me where to dig for His treasures, those pearls of great price. He has also given me the opportunity to share these hidden things with others."

"So how do you determine what to read and what to seek out?" Jonathan asked.

"The Lord always puts it on my heart, or He hands me a particular book and asks me to read it. Once read, we discuss it and He teaches me as He leads me into more of His grace. He uses the old as well as t h e new. Many of the writings of the saints are found in the kingdom, and many, many revisions have been made as they see their errors come to light. I guess it is a continual work in progress," Chuck added jokingly.

"It's funny how the Lord directs our lives according to our gifts. The same gifts we had on earth followed us right on into eternity. It's amazing how our earthly ministries prepared us for heavenly work,"

Jonathan added. "My knowledge is growing more and more as I'm learning so many things about Him. Just to learn of His attributes will take all of eternity. How can I begin to grasp the depths of His love and faithfulness; which reaches deeper than the deepest seas? How can I begin to even scratch the depths of His mercy? I have all of eternity to study the depths of His being; this is grace being built upon grace."

"It's interesting how we're made perfect, and yet God's work in us continues. With great joy and pleasure, we learn more and more without the thorns and thistles of that old world."

"Look at the gift of music that many of the saints had in the old world, and the joy which they had in leading worship. Now it's those very same people who are called to sing the Lord's praises at many of our gatherings, even before the Great Assembly. I'll bet they never expected to continue to learn, practice and grow in their musical gifts?"

---

[33] Proverbs 25:2

Jonathan said, "Look at our other brothers and sisters who had the gift of teaching and preaching and were called to be shepherds of the flock.

Now they are declaring God's wonderful grace in various gatherings all over the kingdom. All of our gifts have followed us into eternity, and we are growing in them as we are called to use them."

Suddenly, a trumpet that could be heard throughout the entire kingdom blasted. It blasted again and then again for a third time. It was the call for the entire kingdom to gather for worship.

At the sound of the trumpet blasts, Jonathan and Chuck headed toward the Great Hall. They traveled the two or three hundred miles quickly. The whole kingdom was on the move, all heading in the same direction.

As they came in sight of the building, Jonathan watched as millions upon millions of people were entering. Chuck tapped Jonathan on the shoulder and motioned for him to look up. A great smile fell upon his face as he watched millions upon millions of angels flying in from every direction of the kingdom. They seem to cover the sky as they flew overhead, and gracefully glided down in order to walk into the great hall and mingle with all the saints.

Chuck and Jonathan walked through the massive wooden doors, which were about fifty feet wide and two hundred feet high. They found their seats in the Great Hall and waited for the service to begin.

The hall was stretched out in every direction farther than any earthly eye could see; even the ceiling seemed endless in height and breadth. People entered in from every direction and found their seats facing a throne that was made of pure gold, which was high and lifted up so that every eye could see it.

The entire kingdom was now seated together, from the lowly pauper to the great kings and queens of old. Whole families sat together, sons and daughters, fathers and mothers, and grandparents to the fifth, sixth, tenth and even fifty generations back. All of God's people throughout the ages were gathered together; no walls of denomination or separation of any kind could be seen. Everyone was there who called on the name of the Lord as their inheritance, and none were disappointed.

Suddenly, a man stepped forward and stood in front of the great assembly. No one wondered who this man was; everyone knew him as the earthly prophet, Moses.

Moses raised his hands and hushed the crowd. Then he cried out in a voice that could be heard clearly and distinctly over the millions of people that gathered in the great hall.

Moses said, [34]"You have not come to that mountain of old which can be touched, that which was burning with fire; to darkness, gloom and storm; to a trumpet blast or to such a voice speaking words that those who heard it begged that no further word be spoken to them, because they could not bear what was commanded: 'Back then at Mount Sinai, if even an animal touched the mountain, it was stoned.' 'The sight was so terrifying that I said, 'I am trembling with fear.'"

Moses stepped back, and another man stepped forward whom everyone knew was the Apostle Paul; he raised his hands and cried out, [35]"But you have come to Mount Zion, to the heavenly Jerusalem, the city of the living God. You have come to thousands upon thousands of angels in joyful assembly, to the church of the firstborn, whose names are written in Heaven. You have come to God, the Judge of all men, to the spirits of righteous men made perfect, to Jesus, the mediator of the new covenant, and to the sprinkled blood of Jesus that speaks a better word than the blood of Abel."

Suddenly, from the throne came a brilliant dazzling light that flooded the entire assembly. High above, somewhere in the expanse of the endless ceiling, came flashes of lightning followed by cracks of thunder; every eye looked up at the amazing display of God's mighty power.

Then, a long trumpet blast sounded from the four corners of the massive hall and four heavenly creatures came forward and declared in a loud voice, [36]"He who sits on the Throne is the

---

[34] Hebrews 12:18-21
[35] Hebrews 12:22-24
[36] Revelation 5:13

Light of the World, and His gospel has been proclaimed to every creature under Heaven. He is the Lamb of God who took away the sins of the world, the Blessed One. He is the Stone the builders rejected, but He has become The Capstone, The Cornerstone and all the heavens delight in Him. Who is this sitting on the throne? It is the Lion of the Tribe of Judah. He has overcome death and Hades, for He is King of Kings and Lord of Lords, He is our God and Savior; He is Jesus Christ the Lord."

Then, the four living creatures fell down and worshipped. Cheers arose from all over the massive hall. In the distance, a familiar song began to play and the great assembly started to sing. People were standing with their hands lifted high in worship, while others had their eyes closed and their faces were shining with splendor, reflecting the love that was written on their hearts. The worship was alive, real, filled with the Spirit's power. The instruments thundered throughout the hall in perfect unity. The words flowed from the hearts of the heavenly host, like a dam bursting forth and flooding the valleys below. Their praises went up like sweet incense before the throne where the King of the Ages was sitting.

When the song was over, the Lord Himself stepped down from the Throne, and His presence seemed to fill the entire hall. As He began to speak, His voice reminded Jonathan of the sound of gentle waves rolling onto the seashore. His voice was so gentle and peaceful to every heart, so much so that a great peace enveloped their very being.

He said, "Welcome my beloved, [37]my treasured possession; you are [38]my garden of delight. [39]I have loved you with an everlasting love; I have drawn you with loving-kindness. You are the church, my bride, and I presented you to myself [40]as a radiant church, without stain or wrinkle or any other blemish; you are holy and blameless.

---

[37] Deuteronomy 7:6
[38] Isaiah 5:7
[39] Isaiah 31:3
[40] Isaiah 43:1-3

"I fulfilled all my good promises, [41]for I have redeemed you. I   have summoned you by name; you are mine. When you passed through the waters, I was with you; and when you passed through   the rivers, they did not sweep over you. When you walked through the fire, you did not get burned; the flames did not set you ablaze, for I   am the Lord, your God, the Holy One of Israel, and your Savior.

"Consider the mold from which you came. [42]From the very beginning I created the heavens and the earth. [43]I created man in my own image. I blessed him and said, [44]'Be fruitful and increase in number; fill the earth and subdue it. Rule over the fish of the sea and the birds of the air and over every living creature that moves on the ground.' [45]I saw everything that I had made, and it was very good.

"In the beauty of my creation, a dark blackness dawned and evil crept in. Your vanquished enemy, that [46]ancient serpent, the devil, Satan, entered in and deceived your first parents causing them to sin and rebel against me, their Fountain of Delight.

"Sin then entered in their hearts and enslaved them. The chains of death began to hold them fast, but a remedy was already in my heart. Sin did not stop at the garden, but it spread like a wildfire and entered the heart of every man, woman and child throughout the ages. From that first sin, the river of death and separation began.   It caused [47]all mankind to sin and fall short of my glory.

"From the beginning, I watched [48]how great man's wickedness on the earth had become, so that every inclination of the thoughts of his heart was evil. I was grieved that I had created man on the earth, and my heart was filled with great sadness. So, I said, 'I will wipe mankind, whom I have created, from the face of the earth—men and animals, and creatures that move along the ground,

---

[41] Isaiah 43:1-3
[42] Genesis 1:1
[43] Genesis 1:27
[44] Genesis 1:28
[45] Genesis 1:31
[46] Revelation 20:2
[47] Romans 3:22-23
[48] Genesis 6:5-8

and the birds of the air—for I am grieved that I have made them. But Noah found favor in my eyes.'

"Like Noah, who sits before you today, you also have found favor in my eyes. It was in my heart to save, to redeem, to love and to make right what was wrong, for you are my very own. It was my desire and great pleasure to pursue you, in spite of your sins, for I am your redeemer and friend.

"My call of repentance and the forgiveness of sins started in ancient times, and continued right up to the day of my coming. I was calling a people to be my very own, my treasured possession, a people that would [49]love the Lord their God with all their heart, soul and mind.

"My call for repentance and forgiveness went out into the whole world, and [50]this is the gospel that you have heard and that which has been proclaimed to every creature under Heaven. [51]Even from the creation of the world, my invisible qualities—my eternal power and divine nature—have been clearly seen, being understood from what has been made, so that men are without excuse.

"Even though creation declared and my gospel called, men refused to repent, so my own hand worked salvation for them. [52]On the day of your salvation, I am the one who helped you. I brought you into my kingdom, my church, as a safe haven and rescued you from the power of darkness, the bondage of sin and I drew you out of Satan's dominion.

"From the beginning, my people had been tormented by the wickedness of the world around them and the evil schemes of the devil. "Consider my faithful servant Lot, who also stands before you today. He also had to deal with the filth of sin. He was [53]a righteous man, who was distressed by the filthy lives of lawless men. He was a righteous man and he lived among them day

---

[49] Luke 10:27
[50] Colossians 1:23
[51] Romans 1:20
[52] 1 Corinthians 6:2
[53] 2 Peter 2 7-8

after day.

He was tormented in his righteous soul by the lawless deeds he witnessed and heard.

"Consider my faithful servant David, another who stands before you now. He also suffered because of the sin that plagues the hearts of men. He was often surrounded by wicked men, and he truly suffered in his body and soul. I moved in him, and by my hand he wrote many psalms regarding the afflictions he himself went through which testify to the cruelty of mankind. Listen to the words of his mouth, the prayers of his lips, when in great tribulation, he cried out to me:

[54] "'Deliver me from my enemies, O my God; protect me from those who rise up against me. Deliver me from evildoers and save me from bloodthirsty men. See how they lie in wait for me! Fierce men conspire against me for no offense or sin of mine, O Lord. I have done no wrong, yet they are ready to attack me. Arise to help me; look on my plight!'"

The Lord began to walk forward, and Jonathan watched Him cross what seemed to be a sea of deep blue glass in front of His throne. His walk was that of a Majestic King, high and exalted, and the train of His robe flowed behind Him, and it seemed to cover the sea of glass.

He noticed that high above the Lord seraphs were flying, each of them had six wings: With two wings they covered their faces and with two they covered their feet, with the other two they were flying.

They cried out "Holy, holy, holy is the Lord Almighty; the whole earth is full of His glory." At the sound of their voices the doorposts and thresholds shook and the hall was filled with smoke. As quickly as the smoke came, it began to rise up toward the endless ceiling and it then disappeared into the great expanse.

As He walked across the sea of glass, suddenly the Father appeared beside his Son, and they walked together. As they were walking, fire and wind seemed to flow out from the both of them and it surround them, as if it were a part of them.

---

[54] Psalm 59:1-4

At that point, all of heaven was silent and no movement could be seen in the entire hall. Everyone watched as the Father, Son, and Holy Ghost crossed the sea of glass and stopped before the great multitude.

Jonathan thought, "There is no way to describe what I am witnessing; it is beyond my comprehension." He knew he could never describe what it was like seeing the fullness, completeness and oneness of the Triune Godhead to any earthly bound human.

The Great Shepherd of the Sheep spoke with gentle words and with great compassion.

He said, "The wicked of that world had also laid a trap for me." As he said this, he pulled back the sleeves of his majestic robe and showed the great congregation the scars the nails had made.

Jonathan whispered, "His love would have held Him there." He then showed the scars the whips had made.

Someone next to Jonathan whispered. [55]"By his stripes, we are healed."

He then showed the scars upon his brow that the crown of thorns had made.

Then many of the saints said quietly, [56]"It should have been the royal one, made of jewels and gold instead." He then showed the scar on his side, the one that the spear had made.

The whole congregation whispered, [57]"They will look upon the one they have pierced."

The Lord spoke quietly, and the words seemed to press themselves on every heart. "It was my great desire and delight to save, and it was in my heart to redeem you with a mighty hand. I want you to know [58]that no one took my life from me, but I laid it down freely of my own accord. I had the authority to lay it down and the authority to take it up again. I gave myself willingly, into their hands, and they did all that they desired to the Son of Man. If this is how they treated me, your Lord, they certainly have treated you in

---

[55] Isaiah 53:5
[56] Michael Card, The song 'Why'
[57] John 19:37
[58] John 10:18

the same way.

"The wicked have always stood against the righteous, and even pursued them to death.

Consider my servant, Steven, who stands before you now. They persecuted him and stoned him. They have persecuted my people throughout the ages. Centuries ago, I let my faithful servant, John, see the [59]souls under the altar; those who had been slain because of the Word of God and the testimony they had maintained. John saw them and heard them cry out, "'How long, Sovereign Lord, holy and true, until you judge the inhabitants of the earth and avenge our blood?' "I then gave them white robes, and told them to wait a little longer, until the number of their fellow servants and brothers who were to be killed as they had, had been completed.

"Finally, the day of my promise came, the day of relief, the day of my coming. It was a day that will be in your hearts and minds for eternity. For it was the day I fulfilled my promise to return and take you where I am. It was a day of vengeance for the wicked and a day of salvation for the righteous.

"Many of you saw way too much suffering, and you prayed that I [60]would take the earth by the edges and shake the wicked out of it. I answered those prayers the day I returned. Justice has been paid in full to the wicked, and reconciliation has been given in full to the righteous."

'I said to you then, [61]'Do not let your hearts be troubled. Trust in God; trust also in me. In my Father's house are many rooms; if it were not so I would have told you. I am going there to prepare a place for you. And if I go and prepare a place for you, I will come back and take you to be with me, that you also may be where I am.'

"I was zealous for that day when you would be with me, and now that day of fulfillment has come. It was the day that I answered all your hopes and dreams.

"My beloved, your prayers were never in vain. I heard all your cries, counted all your tears and I marked down all your

---

[59] Revelation 6:9-11
[60] Job 38:13
[61] John 14:1-3

afflictions. Nothing you went through escaped my loving gaze. It was always in my heart to free you completely from all the pains of that fallen world. I wanted to remove the sadness, loneliness and affliction you encountered from the snares of that old world.

All of you have this in common; in your sadness, loneliness and pain you have loved me and remained faithful till the end.

"My desire has always been to join all my people together, the saints in the heavenly kingdom with the saints in the earthly kingdom. I wanted to open the shepherd's gate and lead my sheep into their eternal dwelling, making them into one-fold, one church and one kingdom. It was also your heavenly Father's desire to unite the church, for He desires to lavish on you the riches of the kingdom, for you are His beloved children.

"When I came for you, my bride, it indeed was a great and glorious day. I found many of you ready with your lamps trimmed and burning, while others were not prepared and [62]escaped through the flames. I am the bridegroom and you are my beloved bride, and I have carried you home to be by my side.

"You can see today that I have never abandoned you, but that I protected and cared for you until the very end. [63]I have given you eternal life and I promised you would not perish and that no one could snatch you out of my hands. When you wandered away, I pursued you; when you fell, I picked you up and carried you with my everlasting arms, holding you close to my heart. I pursued you because I love you; you are mine and I am yours."

There was a pause for a moment, during which Jesus looked out among the vast multitude. He let His eyes slowly move over them. Everyone had the sensation that He was looking at each of them personally. They saw in His eyes a love that they knew could never be extinguished. His eyes spoke silently to each and every person, telling each of them that they were accepted in the beloved.

Jesus then raised His hands and blessed the multitude. As He did this, His countenance began to change with an ever-

---

[62] 1 Corinthians 3:15
[63] John 10:28

increasing glory. The Father's love also burst forth and was shining like the noonday sun. Their glory continued to grow brighter and brighter, and it began to flood the massive hall with a dazzling white light that not only could be seen but felt. Everything and everyone were illuminated by His glory, even the great heights of the expanse above grew brighter and brighter. They slowly began to rise above the great assembly. Every hand was raised to block the brightness of the light, and every eye squinted as the glory increased. They all watched as the Lord rose higher, higher and higher."

Wind and fire suddenly came forth from their presence and filled the entire assembly. The Holy Spirit took what was said and seen, and began applying it to the hearts of the people."

With a final parting word, the Lord said, "Go forth and share with each other, what you heard today. Share with each other your stories about the great and glorious day of the Lord. Remember to entertain strangers, your brothers and sisters you have not yet met. You will hear one amazing story after another."

Music began quietly and grew slowly in intensity. Jonathan began to sing a familiar song and as he sang, the Holy Spirit moved him to sing with his whole heart and soul. It was as if the Spirit, Himself, was singing from somewhere deep within him.

Their songs of praise rose up before the throne like a fragrant offering, holy and pleasing to the Lord.

As the service ended, it seemed that every mind was turned to where they were at the Second Coming. Jonathan knew that millions and millions of stories were about to be told. Many people would be gathering with families, friends and strangers. Jonathan left the massive hall and wondered with whom he would be sharing his story.

Chapter 6: Gathering behind the King

Jonathan made his way out of the massive hall. All around him walked millions of his brothers and sisters who each had their own stories to tell regarding that Great Day. Even angels had stories to tell. Jonathan heard some of these angelic stories first-hand; he had often fellowshipped with many of them in the kingdom. One angel told him that the Son of Man had sent him [64]to weed out of His kingdom everything that caused sin and all who did evil. He was told to separate the wicked from the righteous. [65]While from other angels he heard that they were sent to gather His elect from the four winds, from one end of the heavens to the other. Everyone had his or her own stories, from the least to the greatest, and Jonathan had his own story as well.

As he was making his way home, a man ran up beside him and tapped him on the shoulder.

"Hi Jonathan, my name is William. The Lord sent me to talk to you about the Second Coming; He said we would both enjoy each other's stories about that great day."

"Hi William, it's a pleasure to meet you. I would love to hear your story," Jonathan said excitedly.

"I'm eager to hear yours as well," William said.

"So, when and where did you live?" Jonathan asked

"I was born in 1857 and I lived in Quebec, Canada. I came here in 1925 to be with the Lord. How about you?" William asked.

"I grew up in Massachusetts, and I was living on earth right up to the day of the Second Coming," Jonathan said.

"We are going to have two very different perspectives; mine starts in Heaven, while yours starts on Earth." William said this with a big smile on his face.

"Let's take a walk to where our Lord's Throne is and we can talk there, at the beginning of the River of Life. I love the view

---

[64] Matthew 13:41,49
[65] Matthew 24:31

from there; it's awesome." William added.

Jonathan and William headed toward the center of the Kingdom. As they traveled, they shared stories of how the Lord had worked in their lives and in the lives of their families. They both stopped when they came within view of the Throne and its surrounding buildings. It was situated high upon a hill that overlooked the entire kingdom. As they looked up, the road they were on swerved to the left and then the right; all the way up the hill it swerved back and forth. On the road, white arched bridges could be seen where the road crossed the River of Life as it made its way to the summit.

At each bridge they stopped and looked down upon the water as it cascaded to the valley below.

They finally made it to the summit, and walked over to some benches that were placed beside the river as it broke over the crest of the hill. It was an awesome sight with the Throne of God behind them, and ahead of them the river flowed over a cliff, dropping hundreds of feet below. The river continued down the hill swerving back and forth, continuing through the city, and then out the Southern Gate to one of God's hidden chambers in some distant land.

Jonathan said, "So, tell me your story about the Second Coming."

"I remember it vividly. I was with my earthly wife, Cristan, our children, grandchildren and many other saints enjoying ourselves beside the River of Life down near the Emerald Gate. As we were talking, a trumpet blasted once, and then it sounded again, and again, it blasted seven times in all. Then the Lord himself appeared high above and called all the people to gather at the Worship Hall for a special blessing. "Everyone was excited as we made our way there where the rest of the kingdom was gathering. When we were all seated, God the Father stood up and addressed us.

"He said, 'Welcome, my beloved. I have great news that is for all the people. Behold the Day of the Lord is here; we will wait no longer. The Day of reckoning has arrived. It is time to gather my flock from the four corners of the world and judge all nations in righteousness. The day has come to gather and separate the sheep from the goats. Behold, this is a day of great joy and celebration for the righteous, and a day of tribulation for the wicked; for I will strike down the nations and level every proud peak and raise every humble valley.

"Suddenly a blast of light came from above and caught everyone's attention. In the expanse between the Throne and the endless ceiling, the King of Kings and Lord of Lords came riding on [66]a white horse, and before the throne, the four living creatures cried out, "The rider of the white horse is called faithful and true.

"I watched as the Son of Man flew down on his white horse and landed on the Sea of Glass. He then continued across the Sea of Glass and stopped before the Great Throne. The rider was dressed in fine white linen, an awesome sword hung on his right side that shined and glittered before us all. He wore a majestic robe, which had the words KING OF KINGS AND LORD OF LORDS embroidered in gold. On His head was a crown, which seemed to intersect with many other crowns. His eyes were ablaze, shining forth His power, holiness and righteousness. He drew His sword from its sheath and raised it high for all of us to see.

"The Father watched the Son and said with a voice of authority and command, 'With this sword He will strike down the nations, and I will make His enemies a footstool for his feet.'

"As He said this, the Son swung the sword and brilliant light traced behind it.

"The Father said in a loud voice, 'Behold, The King of Glory, strong and mighty. Now gather behind Him, for the day has come to establish eternal righteousness.'"

Jonathan said, "Wow, I can't image how exciting that must have been. It gives me chills down my spine just thinking of it."

William said, "That day, every heart was captured, and excitement filled the entire kingdom. But there is more, much more to tell."

"I watched as the Lord Jesus turned His horse and it

---

[66] Revelation 19:11-16

raced across the Sea of Glass, stopping half way. From out of every corner of the assembly the angels rose up and flew behind him, and at that moment, the horse railed high in the air and its hoofs landed hard, echoing loudly throughout the massive hall. God the Father then called all the saints to gather, and the Holy Spirit directed us to our positions. Thousands upon thousands of His holy ones gathered behind Him for the great [67]Day of the Lord.

"The Lord Jesus began to move forward through the hall, and we all gathered behind Him. We continued through the city streets until we reached the gate, those ancient doors. Then all of us cried out in unison,

[68]'Lift up your heads, O you gates; be lifted up, you ancient doors, for the King of Glory is coming, who is this King of Glory? The Lord strong and mighty, the Lord mighty in battle.'

The gates of the kingdom were opened and we marched out with the Lord. The sight around me was amazing, a great host of thousands upon thousands of times ten thousand left the City of our God to participate in the [69]Great and Dreadful Day of the Lord.

"We traveled for a time, making our way to the earth. We could have been there in a moment, but I believe the Lord wanted our anticipation and excitement to build. Finally, we were above the clouds of earth. We covered the entire sky, and in fact, we covered the entire globe of the earth. We were all looking down upon that Old World, waiting and waiting, and then suddenly the long-awaited trumpet blast of God was sounded. The sound was so intense that the earth shook violently under its power. Mountains crumbled and valleys were raised up, some rivers seemed to vanish as parts of the earth gave way; even the heavens themselves seemed to shake like leaves on a tree.

There was a pause for a moment as William reflected on that day, and he closed his story with this statement. "I watched as the whole earth was awakened from its slumber, and you know what happened after that. Now tell me your story."

---

[67] Joel 2:31
[68] Psalm 24:7-8
[69] Joel 2:31

Chapter 7: The Second Coming

Jonathan exclaimed, "Oh, what a day! What an unexpected and glorious day. I thought it was going to be one of the worst days of my life. I was expecting a day of extreme stress and sadness on my part, with tears of disappointment and anger on the part of my employees. It started months before, when the economy in that old world plummeted. I was a co-owner of a company and sales were drying up, everyone was hurting everywhere. It was a slow downhill spiral and finally we hit rock bottom. We finally made the decision to let everyone go. These were my friends, people whom I had worked with for many, many years.

"I remember that day so vividly, with such great detail. I remember waking up tired, not wanting to get out of bed because of the sleepless night I had. I moved slowly that morning, and finally started off on my thirty-five-minute drive to work. I was in no great rush; I drove slowly because I was dreading what was to come. We had to tell a group of friends that we were laying them off. I knew they saw it coming, but it still didn't make it easy, I felt as if I had failed them. I was praying fervently that it would go well, but I knew it was going to be a very long, stressful, miserable day.

"I remember taking the final turn down the street and seeing my building in the distance. I turned into the parking lot and just sat there looking at the old brick building, not wanting to go in. I finally turned off the car engine and started across the parking lot, dreading every step of the way as I headed toward the front door. Halfway across the parking lot I heard a trumpet blast that was so loud and powerful that it shook the ground under me, knocking me off balance so that I almost fell to the ground. All around me windows were shattering. Some of the old buildings crumbled and collapsed. The blast was so powerful it made many of the leaves fall from the trees around me. Its sound shook the very depths of my soul. As you know, that trumpet blast was heard all over the entire world.

"I remember quite well the fear that gripped me as I looked up from where the trumpet blast had come. And that is when

I saw these massive dark clouds that seemed to continually roll over themselves, resembling the smoke that comes out of a volcano. The clouds came quickly, moving forward, followed by flashes of lightning and cracks of thunder. That was when I saw the Lord, [70]the Son of Man, riding upon those great clouds. He was high and lifted up and He displayed great, great power and glory. I could also see behind Him thousands upon thousands of His holy ones filling the entire sky; at the sight of them I began trembling.

"I was filled with conflicting emotions. Fear gripped me, for I wondered if I was really ready. Then joy began to overtake me, for I knew I was His. It was exciting and terrifying all at the same time. I seemed to lose all of my ability to do anything; it was almost as if I was frozen in time. Nothing mattered to me anymore; only that very moment. I watched as He came, wondering just what it was that I should do. Should I stand there, bow down, lift my hands, pray, repent, should I call out to Him? I didn't know what to do. The thought entered my mind only for a moment, and that is when I heard the [71]angel's loud trumpet call, and in a flash, in the twinkling of an eye, I was changed.

"I was no longer the same. The old man was gone and the new man emerged. That body of mine that was sown to perish was raised imperishable. That body of mine that was sown in dishonor and weakness was raised in glory and power. That perishable and mortal side of me fell away, just like rotten clothes. I became a new creation, taking on my new heavenly body that is imperishable and immortal. Then the saying that is written came true: [72]'Death has been swallowed up in victory.' I did not have to taste death, for my King tasted death for me.

"In a flash, the twinkling of an eye, I found myself caught up in the clouds with the Lord. As I appeared there, my brothers and sisters welcomed me with great smiles and excitement. Every one of the saints that was on the earth was caught up at the same time. We all gathered together behind the King of Kings and Lord of Lords to

---

[70] Matthew 24:30
[71] 1 Corinthians 15:52-55
[72] 1 Corinthians 15:42

participate in that great and awesome day, The Day of the Lord."

Jonathan stopped talking for a moment, and William could tell that he was in deep thought. Finally, he said, "So there I stood, a sinner saved by grace, standing in the company of the upright, with the Lord Jesus Christ in front of me"

William added, "That was a truly wonderful moment. When we were all gathered together, having all of God's people joined together made that day feel so complete. The Lord knew this would be a wonderful blessing for all of us under one victorious banner.

"It was also a very sad day of weeping and wailing for the rest of the people of the earth who had rejected the Lord and did not receive his merciful invitation of eternal life. They [73]saw the Son of Man sitting at the right hand of the Mighty One and coming on the clouds of heaven. And they could do nothing about the outcome. Their time had come and they didn't accept Him.

"At the sight of Him and the entire heavenly host, all the peoples that were left on the earth were scattered. The rich, the poor, the young and old, all of them were scattered. I watched as they tried to [74]hide in caves and among the rocks of the mountains. I even heard some of them cry out asking that the mountains and the rocks would fall on them. They didn't want to see or be confronted with the face of Him who sits on the throne, and from the wrath of the Lamb that was sure to come!"

Jonathan added, "From above, all the people looked like ants scurrying this way and that. Some were hiding, some were crying and weeping, and others were gripped by a fear that paralyzed them. For the great day of God's wrath had come, and who can stand?"

William added, "On that day I saw great mourning, disappointment and terrible fear for all who were left on the earth. [75]I watched while all the nations of the earth mourned, every eye saw Him, even those who pierced Him; and all the peoples of the earth mourned because of Him. The Day of the Lord had come with

---

[73] Mathew 26:64
[74] Revelation 6:15-16
[75] Revelation 1:7

a vengeance, and He was [76]destroying all dominion, authority and power. He was finally putting all His enemies under His feet!"

Jonathan added, "Finally the end came, when God sent out His angels to harvest the earth and gather all mankind for the Day of Judgment. None could escape. [77]I remember the voice that called to all those who were in their graves to, rise and they came forth. [78]I watched as the sea gave up the dead that were in them. And then, I watched Death and Hades give up the dead that were in them. Each person was about to be judged according to what he had done, according to God's holy standard, not man's."

William said, "That day will never be forgotten in Heaven or in Hell. It will be remembered for all of eternity."

As they were sitting, a trumpet blasted and the call to gather was heard throughout the kingdom.

---

[76] 1 Corinthians 15:24-25
[77] John 5:28-29
[78] Revelation 20:13

Chapter 8: The Promise Fulfilled

J onathan and William were making their way back to the massive hall. They both felt that their stories were not complete and that many other hidden things happened on that great day. They looked forward to what the Lord himself would reveal. They knew that the Lord's message would add closure to their stories.

Everyone in the kingdom was on the move; great excitement and anticipation could be seen on the faces of the people who surrounded them. They were about to know things that were hidden from man before the foundations of the world and their excitement continued to build.

They made their way to their seats and they watched as millions and millions of people took their places in the great assembly.

Jonathan leaned over to William and said, "You know, I recognize a few thousand faces, but there are still millions upon millions of people I still don't know."

"I know exactly what you mean, but we have all of eternity to meet them. I hope that is long enough," William laughed.

Finally, everyone was seated and they were all waiting upon the Lord. Suddenly [79]there came a great and powerful wind that tore through the great hall toward the throne, but the Lord was not in the wind. After the wind, there came a great and awesome earthquake that shook the foundations of the massive hall. Everyone expected to see the Lord, but the Lord was not in the earthquake. After the earthquake, there came a great and all-consuming fire that flew forward toward the throne, but the Lord was not in the fire. After the fire there came a gentle whisper that proceeded toward the throne. And then the Lord of Hosts appeared before the great assembly.

---

[79] 1 kings 19:11-13

Jonathan felt a great peace and calmness come over him; it was a peace that surpassed all his understanding. He knew that peace came when the Spirit of God brushed past him in that gentle wind or whisper. The whole assembly felt the same way. For the wind or whisper came from every direction as it approached the throne, and peace fell upon all who were there.

Then the Lord began to speak. "You have heard many amazing stories as you shared with each other where you were and what you saw upon that Great Day. I myself have a few things to share that many of you may not have considered. [80]I have made many great and precious promises to restore everything that I have promised long ago through my holy prophets and the Word."

"Think of that great enemy, that destroyer of life, the one called death. From the very beginning, it struck fear in the hearts of all mankind. Death separated husband from wife, children from parents, and friends from friends. Death robbed, destroyed and laid siege to many hearts. I have heard all the cries of the brokenhearted and the weeping that continued throughout the night. The grave was never satisfied and it never said, 'Enough.' So, death continued right up to the Great Day of my coming. But now death has been vanquished and it cannot be found. I promised that death would be swallowed up in victory and my promise has been fulfilled.

"Think also of my creation and the frustration that it was subjected to. Consider the simple things like [81]the grass and flowers of the fields, and ow the wind blew upon them and they were gone, and how its place remembered them no more.

Consider the animals that suffered because of man's wickedness when I [82]flooded the earth centuries ago. Every living thing that moved on the earth perished— birds, livestock, wild animals, all the creatures that dwelled upon the earth, and all of mankind. Everything on dry land that had the breath of life in its nostrils died. Some would accuse me of not caring for all of my

---

[80] 2 Peter 2 :14
[81] John 14:2-3
[82] Genesis 7:20-22

creation, but I say to you, [83]did I not care for the ravens? They didn't sow or reap; they had no storerooms or barns, yet   I fed them all. [84]Do I not care for all of my creation? For every animal of the forest is mine, as well as the cattle on a thousand hills. I know every bird in the mountains, and the creatures of the field are mine. I had in my heart to make right that which was wrong. Creation groaned and I desired to lift that terrible yoke that was upon it. That is another reason why I delayed my coming no longer.

"Consider the [85]land; it was also affected by the fall. For I said to Adam, 'Cursed is the ground because of you; through painful toil you will eat of it all the days of your life. It will produce thorns and thistles for you and you will eat the plants of the field. By the sweat of your brow you will eat your food until you return to the ground, since from it you were taken; for dust you are and to dust you will return.' My creation itself groaned over sin and was in bondage to decay and death. The whole creation has been groaning since the beginning of the fall. For sin did not only affect mankind, but its roots went deep into my Creation. The whole of creation has been suffering right up to the time that I redeemed all things by my return.

"You have heard many great and precious promises made to you, and it was in my heart to fulfill them. You have heard it said, [86]"in my Father's house there are many rooms; if it were not so, I would   have told you. I am going there to prepare a place for you. And if I go and prepare a place for you, I will come back and take you to be with me, that you also may be where I am.' That promise was seared into your hearts and you dreamed of my coming back for you, with great joy you waited expectantly for my return.

[87]I also wanted to be glorified in you, my holy people, and to be marveled at among you that believe. That day was a great day, for your hearts were lifted up in praise. Your spirit soared the

---

[83] Luke 12:24
[84] Psalm 50:10-12
[85] Genesis 3:17-19
[86] Genesis 3:17-19
[87] 2 Thessalonians 1:10

day I came back for all that dwelt upon the earth. By you, my name had been glorified among the nations on that great day.

"That day caught many by surprise. Many of you wondered if I would ever really return, because it seemed such a long time from my earthly ministry to that Great Day of my second coming.

"As you now know, [88]I am not slow in keeping my promises, as some may understand slowness. I was patient with you, not wanting anyone to perish, but desiring everyone to come to repentance. The Day of the Lord came like a thief in the night and, as you remember, the heavens disappeared with a roar; the elements were destroyed by fire, and the earth and everything in it was laid bare.

"After that came The Great Judgment. As you have all witnessed, [89]"all mankind appeared before the Judgment Seat of Jesus Christ, and each one received what was due him for the things done while in the body, whether good or bad.

"At that point, the Lord Jesus appeared at the Father's side, and He was dressed in Shepherd's Clothes and carried a staff and said, 'That Day of Judgment came and went. You are here with me today dressed in white, and you all received your rewards for the things you had done in the body. For I am the Faithful Shepherd, [90]I stood at the door and knocked, and you heard my voice and opened the door. Then, I came in and ate with you and you with me. For when I was hungry you gave me something to eat, when I was thirsty you gave me something to drink, and when I was a stranger you invited me in.'

"You have all passed through many hardships in my name. [91]And now you are blessed by my Father and you have taken your inheritance, the kingdom prepared for you since the creation of the world.'

---

[88] 2 Peter 3:9-10
[89] 2 Corinthians 5:10
[90] Revelation 2:7
[91] Matthew 25:34-35

[92]"You are my beloved, for my Father gave you ears to hear what the Spirit said to the churches. You have overcome and I have given you the right to eat from the tree of life. [93]Many of you were faithful, some even to the point of death, and I have given you the crown of life. You truly [94]overcame and you were not hurt at all by the second death. I have given you some of the hidden manna that I have promised. I have also given you a white stone with a new name written on it, known only to you and me. I said to you in those days, 'He who overcomes will be dressed in white and I will never blot out his name from the book of life, but will acknowledge your name before my Father and his angels'. This I did for all of you on that Great Day.'

"I also said, [95]"To him who overcomes, I will make him a pillar in the temple of my God. Never again will he leave it, and I will write on him the name of my God and the name of the city of my God, the New Jerusalem. You saw with your own eyes the city coming down out of heaven from your Heavenly Father. All these promises and blessings have been showered down upon you, for you have overcome. [96]I have also given you the right to sit with me on my throne, just as I overcame and sat down with my Father on His throne. So, you are with me today and have not left my side. And you will never ever be cast away, for you are mine and I am yours and I am your great reward. All of these blessings are proof that I have always loved you and that I prepared this place for you."

At this point, the great assembly broke out in worship and lifted holy hands to the Great King. And they sang an old song of praise from the old world.

They sang, [101]"Majesty, worship His majesty; Unto Jesus be all glory, honor, and praise. Majesty, kingdom authority, Flow from His throne unto His own, His anthem praises. So, exalt, lift up on high the name of Jesus. Magnify, come glorify Christ Jesus, the

---

[92] Revelation 2:7
[93] Revelation 2:10-11
[94] Revelation 2:11
[95] Revelation 3:12
[96] Revelation 3:21

King. Majesty, worship His majesty, Jesus who died, now glorified, King of all Kings."

The praise and worship continued song after song. And new sounds came from new heavenly instruments that were built by the music players. The instruments added a variety of beautiful sounds to the worship. As the singing was coming to a close, three men dressed all in white stepped forward and a hush came over the crowd. Jonathan did not know who they were, but waited in expectation to see what was going to happen.

The men carried two huge bronze cymbals in each of their hands. They lifted them up, slammed them together, and the sound went out like a wave, and it swept over the whole assembly. One of the three lifted his hands and said, [102]"I will extol the Lord at all times; His praise will always be on my lips. Glorify the Lord with me; let us exalt His name together. Those who look to Him are radiant; their faces are never covered with shame. Taste and see that the Lord is good; blessed is the man who takes refuge in Him.

"Fear the Lord, you His saints, for those who fear Him lack nothing. The eyes of the Lord were on the righteous, and His ears were attentive to their cry. The righteous cried out, and the Lord heard them; He delivered them from all their troubles.

"The Lord was always close to the brokenhearted. He saved those who were crushed in spirit. Righteous men may have many troubles, but the Lord has delivered them from them all. The Lord redeemed you, His servants; no one was ever condemned who took refuge in Him."

Jonathan noticed that the men slammed the cymbals together at particular times throughout the discourse, and he could clearly see that the cymbals added meaning to the words when they clashed. Suddenly, a bright light came from the throne and encompassed the Father and the Son. It grew brighter and brighter and expanded out further and further to the outer most expanse of the massive hall. Everyone could feel the awesome warmth, power, and glory of the Holy Spirit as His radiance enveloped all the worshippers. Finally the Lord Jesus raised His arms high and He blessed His people and dismissed them by saying these words: [97]"I was the one who was able to keep you from falling and to present you before my glorious presence without fault and with great joy—I am the only God, your Savior, all glory, majesty, power and authority belongs to me before all of the ages, now and forevermore! Amen."

Not a sound could be heard as everyone contemplated these familiar words that were heard anew in the kingdom.

As Jonathan was leaving, he ran into his youngest son, Ben. They embraced each other and Jonathan asked Ben, "Who were the men with the symbols?"

Ben responded, "They were Heman, Asaph and Ethan." Jonathan had a confused look on his face, and Ben could not help playing into it.

"Come on, you don't know who [98]Heman, Asaph and Ethan are?" Ben said teasing his dad. "You should know them. Maybe if you read your Bible more back then you would know who they were," he said with a smirk.

"Okay, I will tell you. They wrote many of the psalms in the scriptures. They were the musicians David used in the worship when the ark of God was brought back into Jerusalem. They were in charge   of the bronze cymbals in the worship of God. Ethan and Heman were also very, very wise men in their day, for the scriptures even mentioned their wisdom. Remember these words about Solomon?

[99]"Solomon's wisdom was greater than the wisdom of all the men of the East, and greater than all the wisdom of Egypt. He was wiser than any other man, including Ethan the Ezrahite—wiser than Heman, Calcol and Darda, the sons of Mahol. And his fame spread to all the surrounding nations.' Notice Ethan and Herman are among the men listed."

Jonathan looked at his son and said, "Impressive!" Ben laughed and said, "Mom told me."

---

[97] Jude 1:24-25
[98] 1 Chronicles 15:19
[99] 1 kings 4:29-31

They walked out together displaying God's faithfulness for scriptures declaring, [100]"This promise is for you and your children, and for all who are far off —for all whom the Lord our God will call."

As they left the assembly, they embraced again. As Jonathan was walking away, he waved goodbye and headed to his home. But the Lord had other plans he did not know about.

---

[100] Acts 2:39

Chapter 9: The New Jerusalem

A s the days blended into months, months into years and years into centuries, abundant life continued in the Heavenly Kingdom. Every day was different; boredom never set in because every day was filled with wonderful new things to learn, to see and to do.

Heaven was like seeing the ocean for the first time with the waves breaking upon the shore, or being in the desert far away from the city lights and seeing the beauty and vastness of the night sky. Such was the life that Jonathan Stone lived in His eternal kingdom.

One day when Jonathan was home, he heard a knock at his door. As he opened the door, there stood a man he didn't recognize. The man reached out his hand and said, 'Hello Jonathan, my name is Tim. The Lord has sent me here to meet you."

Jonathan reached out, shook his hand saying, "Come on in Tim, and let's get to know each other."

They walked over and sat opposite each other at the dining room table. Jonathan had various fruit and vegetables laid out between them in a decorative fashion.

Tim was the first to speak, "So Jonathan, where did you live in the Old World, and in what century did you live in?"

"I was born in 1962, in a city called Holyoke, in Massachusetts, in what was then the United States. How about you Tim, where were you from and when did you live?"

A huge smile broadened on Tim's face as he said, "I was also born in Holyoke, Massachusetts. I was born in 1965."

"I grew up on Locust Street." Jonathan said with a look of extreme curiosity showing on his face.

"So, did I, what was your house number?"

Both of them began grinning ear to ear, and their eyes were beginning to open wider and wider, wondering what their connection might be.

"I grew up on 181 Locust Street, how about you?" Jonathan inquired. "I lived on 177 Locust Street for the first seven years of my life."

They both let out a long breath and wondered what was coming up next. They continued to look at each other as they each searched their past.

"I wonder," Jonathan said with a distant look on his face. "When I was a little boy, I remember seeing another boy who was in a yard a couple of houses up the street. We introduced ourselves and we played together just that one afternoon. After we were done playing, he asked me if I wanted to come over to his house for supper and then read the Bible. I thought back then that it was kind of cool and weird. After that day I never saw him or played with him again."

Tim jumped in and said, "That was me. I remember playing with you and then asking you to come over for supper. My parents always had a short devotional after supper."

They both looked at each other in amazement and began laughing.

Jonathan said, "I remembered that brief encounter throughout my earthly life, especially after I got saved. I always wondered who that boy was and what had happened to him. Did he move far away or did he stay close because I never saw him again after that."

"The Lord was involved in each of our lives, even way back then when we were children. What we forgot as a chance encounter has been written in the journals of heaven," Tim added.

"It's amazing how the little things that happen in our old lives, things that we forgot or thought were not important, turn out to be the things the Lord brings to the forefront," Jonathan said.

Jonathan and Tim then talked about their earthly lives and the different ways the Lord had impacted each of them. It was a sweet time of fellowship and their conversation brought great joy to each of their hearts; it was a time of mutual encouragement.

Tim said, "I'm in the mood for a walk. I have wanted to explore the eastern part of the Kingdom, near the East Gates. Are you interested in joining me?

"To the east we go." Jonathan said.

As they walked along the Streets of Gold heading towards the eastern gates of the Heavenly Kingdom, Jonathan's mind went back to the first time he saw the Holy City. It felt like it happened moments ago, and he could remember everything in vivid detail. He knew it would always be like that, for he was made anew with a perfect body, soul and mind suited for Him living in eternity.

As they walked the streets of gold beside the River of Life, the road they were looking for appeared ahead of them. At the beginning of the street was a decorative bronze pole with a sign mounted on top that said, "Emmanuel's Highway-East". They began walking down a cobblestone street made of various colored stones. The stones colors matched many of the houses and buildings on the right side of the street as well as the parks and fields on the left side. The colors brought both sides together in perfect harmony.

As they were enjoying their walk, Jonathan asked Tim, "Do you remember the first time the New Jerusalem was revealed?"

"No one will ever forget that day. I remember the Spirit taking us all to that great and high mountain; the whole kingdom was there. I remember when the base of the city suddenly appeared in the heavens above us. Every eye was captivated as the Holy City started descending out of Heaven from God the Father."

Jonathan added, "I remember how God's glory was above the city and the light of His presence shown all around it and illuminated it. It came down from His hands and reminded me of a precious jewel, for the city was as clear as crystal."

Tim added, "I remember that my eyes could barely take in the massive size of the city's foundation and the height of its walls. It was so impressive as it rotated down slowly for all to see. It was like the city was being lowered by an invisible rope that was held in

God's hands. I remember seeing such detail; I could clearly see the [101]twelve foundations and its precious stones with the names of the twelve apostles written on each foundation. I watched as each of the twelve gates of the city rotated in front of me, and I could even see the emblems of the twelve tribes of Israel engraved on each of its gates. I also saw clearly the faces of God's mighty angels standing at attention as each of the gates passed in front of me."

Jonathan said, "It's amazing how God can make a city in the shape of a square or cube so magnificent, beautiful and majestic. The sheer size of the city being lowered from the heavens is still beyond my comprehension.

Think about it; the city is [102]Fourteen hundred miles in width, depth and height, and that is by man's measurements."

Tim added, "I remember how the walls of the city were made of jasper and pure gold. It reminded me of [103]glass glowing in a furnace. The city and its walls were like mirrors, glittering and sparkling from the reflection of God's glory and His awesome presence above it."

"What stands out most of all to me is not the city itself coming down, but it was when I looked up above the city and saw the splendor and majesty of [104]God Almighty and His glory lighting up everything in its path. All the saints had seen Him at the same time and every face seemed to freeze in time as His glory descended on the city and overflowed upon us. I remember grasping for words, just something to express the majesty of what I saw. But no words could be uttered," Jonathan added.

Tim reminisced aloud, "Remember when we used to think the fireworks displays on the 4th of July were amazing? I used to be amazed at the grand finale. I think of the Old World and the best it

---

[101] Revelation 21:14
[102] Revelation 21:16-18
[103] Revelation 21:21
[104] Revelation 21:23

could offer. It's like darkness compared to what we have already seen and what is still to come."

"No comparison at all. It's like comparing the light that comes from a match to the light that comes from the sun," Jonathan added.

Tim continued, "It was funny how we were all grasping for words when suddenly the Lord put a new song in all of our hearts, all at the same time. We sang and lifted up our hands in worship to the one who lit the city with His awesome presence."

Jonathan added, "That's so true. That was such an awesome event. But nothing on that day could ever compare to what happened next. Seeing God's glory is awesome, but hearing His voice was something altogether different. I remember seeing Him rising up from His throne as the city came to rest in its place. I remember Him saying in a loud voice," [105]Now the dwelling of God is with men, and I will live among them. In the midst of all of them, I will be found. You will be my people, and I, myself, will be with you and be your God. I will wipe every tear from your eyes. There is no more death and no more mourning, crying or pain, for I have made the old order of things pass away."

Tim said, almost teary-eyed, "I remember those words very well."

Jonathan added, "I remember the surprise all of us had when the twelve gates of the city suddenly flew open. Every eye was looking down from that high mountain wondering what was going to happen and what was going to come next. Then it came, that loud voice from the throne calling all the saints to enter the city for the first time."

Tim interjected, "That day was majestic. And it was beautiful to see myriads and myriads of the saints from all the ages and centuries flying down the mountain and entering the Holy City through the twelve gates. There was cheering, dancing, and there

---

[105] Revelation 22:3-4

were songs of praise as we entered into our eternal home, our eternal rest, our eternal kingdom; the Kingdom that was prepared for us before the creation of the world.

Watching the Heavenly City, God's glorious presence, His majestic voice and the call to enter the city for the first time still burned fresh in Jonathan's memory. They both praised God as they traveled and reminisced about other events of that day as they made their way to the eastern gates of the kingdom. They traveled a hundred, perhaps even a thousand, miles enjoying each other's company and exploring the city as they went.

Finally, in the distance they could see one of the great eastern walls of the city and it rose high into the clouds. It stood like a mountain in front of them. As they walked closer, they saw one of the Eastern Gates coming within view. They could see the base and capitals of each of the columns of the gates that rose above the walls of the city. On the top of each of the capitals was a large round room with windows facing in every direction, and the roofs were conical in shape as they rose high above the walls.

As they approached the gates, they discovered that the wall of the city was two hundred feet thick and the two gates were fastened to the columns in the exact middle of the wall. The two gates were made out of burnished bronze square posts. The vertical posts were twelve feet apart and rose as high as the eye could see. The horizontal cross-beams blended perfectly into the vertical beams every twelve feet. Fastened between the beams were twelve-foot square hammered gold plates. The plates were identical in size and shape, and they continued up vertical and horizontal as far as the eye could see.

The plates were decoratively engraved with different scenes showing God's mighty acts, from His six days of creation and His day of rest, to His saving power on Israel's behalf. There were plates showing scenes from the plagues in Egypt, to the parting of the red sea, to Joshua crossing the Jordan into the Promise Land. The plates showed Jesus' earthly ministry as well as the Acts of the

Apostles. They showed other events throughout history up to the day of His second coming. Some plates were of well-known historical events while others were of unknown and hidden events, the mysteries of God's saving power in the church throughout history.

As they were admiring the pictures and their great details, Jonathan and Tim realized that they could be there for another hundred years just examining the plates' decorative qualities. They could spend hundreds of years just trying to figure out the mysteries of the Lord's saving power in the lives of the saints throughout the history in the church of the living God. This was just one gate and they still had eleven more to see.

Their little excursion was almost over for now. They knew they had eternity to explore the kingdom, but duties were calling to each of them. They parted ways with a hug, each headed to wherever the Spirit was calling them.

Jonathan was called home, and upon entering he noticed again how his home was made, created and even crafted specifically for him. He remembered how Jesus said [106]"In my Father's house are many rooms; if it were not so, I would have told you. I am going there to prepare a place for you."

Jonathan thought of how his earthly home paled in comparison. Here, everything fit perfectly to who Jonathan became in heaven. He remembered from the Scriptures Jesus saying, [107]"I tell you, use worldly wealth to gain friends for yourselves, so that when it is gone, you will be welcomed into eternal dwellings."

Jonathan had used his earthly wealth for fellowship and for the Kingdom. Now, he was seeing the fruit of his labor, [108]"Where moth and rust do not destroy, and where thieves do not

---

[106] John 14:2
[107] Luke 16:9
[108] Matthew 6:20

break in and steal."

Chapter 10: The Prisoner is Set Free

As time went on and the decades rolled by, Jonathan continued to enjoy the Kingdom that was prepared for him. He was part of it; he was included in it, and he knew it was where he belonged. He always felt at peace here, and he had a great love for everyone in the kingdom. He felt attached to everyone, even though he had met only a fraction of them.

His love continued to grow and grow as the Holy Spirit continued to cultivate the depths of his heart. He also grew in his understanding and had a better grasp of the deep truths of the faith, the faith which he had committed himself to in the old world. One verse that always spoke to his heart was, "I am my lover's and my lover is mine." He first saw the verse engraved on the wedding ring of a friend, and when Jonathan asked him what it meant, his friend said,

"It is a verse from the Song of Solomon, and it means to be joined together, to be as one." That is exactly how Jonathan viewed his position in the kingdom and his love for the Lord of the Kingdom. It was like being a part of an artist's painting, and he was like a brush stroke on the grand canvas of the eternal kingdom.

He did not dwell on that life a lot, but he still loved to see his earthly life through a heavenly perspective. The Shepherd Himself also found great pleasure in showing Jonathan all the great and marvelous things that He had done for him throughout his pilgrimage on earth. So, Jonathan again turned his attention back to those early years.

Jonathan was born in early summer. His parents were James and Amy Stone. He was brought up in a loving family, yet he felt alone. His life felt empty, for the seed of loneliness had taken root deep within his heart.

He was a child that was often in trouble, because he was easily swayed in the wrong directions by his own thoughts and the suggestions of others. He remembered many times when he got in trouble because of the circumstances that he placed himself in. He found that worry, anxiety, fear and heartache were his constant companions, and a great discouragement laid siege upon his heart. In spite of his pain and emptiness, he learned how to suppress his feelings and live with it, and no one was the wiser.

Jonathan remembered the hardest point in his life was in his teen years up to his mid-twenties. This was just before he got saved. As he was thinking of these things, a knock sounded at the door and someone walked in. Jonathan turned and saw his earthly mother, Amy, coming through the door. He got up and gave her a hug, and they both went over to the couches and sat down.

As he looked at her he smiled, for he was always impressed with the power of the [109]new heavenly bodies, compared to the weakness of   the corruptible bodies of the Old World. The earthly bodies were made perishable, sown in weakness and dishonor. They were natural bodies, formed from the dust of the earth, and they bore the image of that first man, Adam. The new heavenly bodies were so different, raised imperishable, filled with glory, power and immortality. The earthly bodies were of one kind, and the new heavenly bodies were of another; they bore the nature of the Man from Heaven, Jesus Christ.

So, Amy's oval face glowed as it reflected the Lord's glory, and   her straight, shoulder-length hair shined with beauty and strength. Her eyes were bright and her demeanor showed forth the new creation, filled with glory, joy, peace and immortality. She moved with grace and elegance as she approached the couch.

As Jonathan saw his mother sitting across from him, he smiled at her and quietly thanked God that many of his earthly relationships had not been severed, but blossomed and continued to grow into a closeness that could never be experienced in the old world. He was so grateful that many relationships he cherished continued and carried on right into eternity.

---

[109] 1 Corinthians 15:42-54

Amy noticed that Jonathan's mind was somewhere else. She smiled and said with a slight grin, "What are you thinking about now?"

They laughed together, for Jonathan knew his mom and she knew him. They could always read each other, which was not lost in glory.

"You are always thinking. So, what's on your mind now?"

"I was just thinking of my teen years and my early twenties and how screwed up I was. It's amazing that the Lord had so much patience with me."

Amy thought for a moment and said with a grin, "I had a lot of patience with you also."

They both laughed, and then Amy said, "Tell me what in particular you were thinking about."

"I remember having a very poor view of myself. I worked very hard to fit in and to be liked by everyone, yet I never really felt that I fit in. I had a lot of friends, but not many good, close friends. I felt I didn't measure up to the standards of other people, as well as my own standards. I said and did many stupid things to try to fi t in, and I never really considered the consequences. I was quick to speak and slow to listen, so my mouth always got me in trouble. I felt like a failure in many ways.

"I remember my marks in school were very low; I always got C's, D's and F's. I never had the discipline to do the things I needed to do. I was always day-dreaming and procrastinating. I could never stay focused, and my grades reflected the person I was. I felt that I didn't have a lot to offer anyone.

"As you remember, I was always overweight and so I got picked on a lot by others. I was the butt of many jokes. I learned to let them roll off of me though. I remember that life was just life, and I lived it day to day. I was always hoping the future had better things in store for me and that my life would change, but I was also fearful that it might not.

"I felt my hope for the future would come by new circumstances in my life. I used to think, 'if only I had a girlfriend, my life would be better.' So my life revolved around finding a girlfriend that would fill what was lacking in my life, to find Miss Right and finally get married and live happily ever after.

"I lived on those words, 'if only.' If only I had a wife. If only I could lose weight. If only I had the perfect job. If only this happened, if only that happened, I would become happy and content. I lived from one high point in life to the next, with big, wide valleys in between. These valleys were always filled with loneliness, sadness and disappointment. I longed for my life to change.

"The best verse that describes my early life and how I sought to change it is Isaiah 55:2, 'Why spend money on what is not bread, and your labor on what does not satisfy? Listen, listen to me, and eat what is good and your soul will delight in the richest of fare.'

"I can relate to this verse because it described who I was. I spent all my energy and efforts on things that in and of themselves did not satisfy the deep longings of my heart. All the things I labored for and poured my energy into, I never got or they slipped through my fingers or it didn't produce the life I expected. Life for me was not satisfying; it was draining, and I always felt unfulfilled. It was as if something was missing deep down in the recesses of my heart."

As Jonathan thought back to those days, he seemed to shudder as he imagined them.

"Praise God, He rescued me from myself. As you know, He did this when I came to faith in my mid-twenties. The Scriptures are so true when they talk about living a new earthly life. It's still amazing that [110]we were buried with Christ in His death through baptism, and when He rose from the dead, we also rose. A new creation came forth that day when I believed: the old was gone and the new had come. I'm so glad that I'll never see or be that poor,

---

[110] Romans 6:3-4

sinful, lonely man again. He was left in the grave, never to rise again."

Amy sat for a moment without saying a word. Finally, she said, "Yes, I understand the pain of loneliness and the strong desires we have for our broken hearts to be healed. Sin seized those moments, and Satan used those opportunities in our lives to lead us down paths that can never satisfy the thirsty soul. Yet love still triumphed. God has always been stronger than our weak hearts, and He has always been able to mend that which was broken. Our hearts were in bondage and deceitful above all things, beyond cure. Who could understand it, but the one who created it is also the one who can fix it – our Great Physician?"

As they were still speaking of these earthly things, the King of Kings and Lord of Lords appeared at their side. They naturally bowed in reverence, without any reluctance. It was so easy to give the Great King the respect and glory due His name when sin was finally vanquished from the human heart.

The Lord asked, "What are you two talking about now?"

They laughed together, for they knew He knew all things from the beginning to the end.

Amy said, "We were just talking about the early days of Jonathan's earthly life."

Jesus said with a smile, "I know them all too well." Jonathan blushed.

Jesus continued, "I know all the struggles that all my people went though, for I know what is inside a man."

Jonathan said, "Thank you, Lord, [117]that you didn't leave me in that state of hopelessness, and that you didn't treat me as my sins deserved, or repay me according to my iniquities."

Jesus said, "Would you like me to tell you what I saw in the deep recesses of your heart and soul?"

Jonathan did not hesitate for a moment; he loved sitting under the teacher's teaching.

As Jesus began to speak, He revealed one mystery after another.

They hung on His every word.

Jesus said to Jonathan, [111]"Even though every inclination of your human heart is evil from childhood and you tried to do everything you could to fill the emptiness, I had barriers set for you. I said, [112]'This far you may come and no farther; here is where your proud waves halt!' You see, Jonathan, your heart craved love from the earliest age. You were willing to do anything to find it and you craved attention also, because you were looking for acceptance. You looked for love and acceptance in the world and found great disappointment instead. I let you roam so you could see and understand that the things of that world could never satisfy the empty human heart.

"Nothing in that old world could ever fill the emptiness that you had. Your heart was dried up and empty and you tried filling it with the things of that world. But no matter how much you tried to fill the emptiness; you were never satisfied. I was the only one that could fill what I left empty. Your heart was made for me and the attention you truly wanted was my acceptance, for I created your innermost being. As you now know, I filled you and made you into a new creation, only after I knew your heart was ready for love. You cannot rush love. I moved your heart and life in a direction that would bring the most fruit to you and others. [113]On the day of Salvation, I helped you. I used tender words to draw your attention."

Jonathan's memory flashed back to those tender words that were given to him. He remembered the cords of love drawing him that day when he gave his life over to the [114]Shepherd and Overseer of his soul.

---

[111] **Genesis 8:21**
[112] Job 38:11
[113] 2 Corinthians 6:1
[114] 1 Peter 2:25

He remembered life changing drastically after that day, [115]for he became born again and he was a new creation in Christ Jesus. It was indeed a great day in that old world when Christ Jesus [123]called him out of darkness into His wonderful light, when the slate of his life was wiped clean and he could begin to live a new life and have a fresh start.

Jesus looked at both of them and embraced them, saying, "My sheep know me, and I know them, [116]for I am my lover's, and my lover is mine."

At this point, Jesus left them.

As they were thinking of what Jesus said, suddenly a burning urge to worship fell over them.

Jonathan and Amy knew at that moment that all the saints, angels and every inhabitant of heaven were being called together to bring their worship to the King of Kings and Lord of Lords. Jonathan and Amy got up in an instant and started on their way to the place of worship.

Gathering for worship was not like it was in the old world. In that world so many things competed for Jonathan's attention: his desire to sleep in, to rest, and to relax. Early in Jonathan's walk everything seemed to be scheduled during Sunday Worship, from family reunions, to holidays and everything in between. He learned early on that a choice had to be made: The Lord, or the competing things of that earthly life. Finally, he made worship his and his family's top priority. Those things that once competed for his time seemed to disappear, and all the family's scheduled things seemed to be rescheduled as time went on. In glory, nothing competed with the Lord's attention. Jonathan loved the worship in heaven; it was always exciting and it filled him with an inexpressible joy.

As they entered the great hall together, excitement started to build. Angels were again flying overhead, and other celestial beings

---

[115] John 3:3
[116] Song of Solomon 6:3

were moving this way and that, to wherever they were called. Smiles were on faces everywhere. Not a single face was downcast, for the old order of things had passed away. Jonathan looked at the Throne with the [117]giant rainbow that encircled it. The rainbow was huge and it reminded him of a beautiful emerald. In a circle around the throne were twenty-four other thrones, and seated on those thrones were the twenty-four elders. They were dressed in white clothes that seemed to glow, and the robes reached down to their feet. Each elder had a golden crown on his head. From the Throne came flashes of lightning that shot out in every direction, and the roaring and crashing of thunder captured everyone's attention. Suddenly seven flaming torches appeared before the Throne, on top of what seemed to be a sea of glass as clear as crystal.

The light of the torches lit up the entire building. The flames reminded Jonathan of a huge bonfire, for the flames reached hundreds of feet into the air. These torches were the seven spirits of God, showing His completeness, and they continued to burn before the Throne.

Then, as always, Jonathan's eyes met the One who redeemed him from sin and death, the One who is called [118]Faithful and True. [119]His eyes were like blazing fire shining forth His righteousness, and on His head were many crowns, for He was the King of All Ages. He was dressed in a robe dipped in blood, showing the full cost of redemption. As Jonathan looked, he saw words written in gold on His robe and on His thigh that said, "King of Kings and Lord of Lords."

Jonathan's heart swelled as he looked and [120]heard the voices of many angels as they encircled the Throne, as well as the living creatures and the elders singing their praises to God. Soon the

---

[117] Revelation 4:3-6
[118] Revelation 3:14
[119] Revelation 19:12-13,16
[120] Revelation 5:11-14

entire congregation was joining in and singing with loud voices.

They sang, "Worthy is the lamb that was slain, to receive power, wealth, wisdom, might and honor, glory and praise!"

Then every creature – in heaven, on earth, under the earth, in the sea, and all that is in them – sang:

"To the one who is seated on the throne and to the Lamb, who is worthy of praise, honor, glory, and ruling power forever and ever!"

Then, in a loud voice that carried over the congregation, the four living creatures said with a voice of command, "Amen," and the elders fell down and worshipped.

At that point, Jonathan began to worship with all his heart. He sang and with freedom lifted his holy hands in praise. He sang new songs and heard all the saints in heaven lifting their voices in one accord.

Jonathan's heart was captured and praise overflowed from it. He was truly satisfied and could see that this was what he was created for.

He remembered worshiping the Lord in the Old World, but it paled in comparison to the heavenly worship. He knew that God, in His goodness, gave His people a small taste of the heavenly worship in the Old World, and he could see that the worship in the Old World prepared him for eternal worship. How long the worship lasted he couldn't tell, but he would be satisfied staying there and continuing forever, throughout eternity. Jonathan wanted to stay right there at the Throne of Grace, but the gathering of worship was ending. Little did Jonathan know that new mysteries were about to be revealed to him.

Chapter 11: The First Murder

As Jonathan was leaving the worship hall, he made his way to Crystal River Park. The park was hundreds and hundreds of miles long, and it followed the River of Life through the entire kingdom. On one side of the park was the river, and on the other side was the city's main street. In some places, the park was only a few hundred feet wide, while in other places it was over twenty miles wide. The park weaved back and forth, always following the river's edge. Sometimes the park was flat for many, many miles, and then suddenly it would rise up higher and higher as it followed the terrain of the hills and mountains of the kingdom. The views were always breath taking, especially when one was high up on a hill or mountainside watching the river and park weave through the valleys below.

As he walked through the park, he came to the place where the mighty trees grow. There were hundreds and hundreds of huge trees rising up seven, eight, nine hundred feet in the air, and their branches spread out like a canopy. Hundreds of people could be found sitting under just one of these giant trees where they soaked in the beauty of their environment and enjoyed the sweet fellowship of each other's company.

Jonathan's excitement grew as he walked past crowds of people that had gathered for fellowship. Some of them had lived in ancient times, others had lived during Christ's earthly ministry, while others lived in Jonathan's generation, and still others lived right up to the day of the coming of the Lord. All types of people were gathering for fellowship with no language barriers, cultures or class differences. The earthly pauper spoke to the earthly king or prince as if he were speaking to his own brother. Earthly slaves enjoined and embraced earthly masters, and they all treasured each other's fellowship.

Jonathan saw daily how God[121]completely removed the pride of man and destroyed that barrier, the dividing wall of hostility that kept people apart. All the inhabitants of heaven were [122]fellow citizens of God's household, which was built on the foundation and teachings of the apostles and prophets, with Christ Jesus, Himself, being the chief cornerstone.

Jonathan oftentimes stopped and talked with the people he met on the way. He did this with freedom and confidence, for they were all one in Christ Jesus. He was never disappointed by a single meeting, but was always blessed by the words, deeds and actions of others. Sometimes he would run into few people, other times he would be with hundreds and even thousands of people who had gathered for fellowship, celebrations, worship and a host of other reasons which had brought them all together. He would enter into worship with them, talk with them, and oftentimes just enjoy getting to know more and more about them. He had no fear of parting company, for the door of fellowship was always open in God's kingdom, and His people continually walked through it.

As Jonathan was walking, he saw two familiar faces in front of him from his past; they reached each other and embraced. Warm loving smiles lighted each of their faces. He stood before an old elder and his wife who had been a part of his church in the old world, but they had moved away when Jonathan was just a babe in Christ.

"Bob and Dot, I knew I would run into you both sooner or later. It's so great to see you two. I missed you guys so much in the old world when you moved back to New Jersey for retirement."

Bob said, "Jonathan, it is truly wonderful to see your face, and I also missed you an awful lot. Consider this, now we can visit and have that sweet fellowship that never can be broken by distance

---

121 Ephesians 2:14
122 Ephesians 2:19-20

again, spoiled by sin or destroyed by the works of the evil one.

"You know what? I really want you to know how God used both of you in my life when I first got saved. You have both spoken many times in my life with your gentleness and your servant-heartedness. I really missed you deeply when you moved away. I always wanted to visit more than that one time, but as you both know, distance was a real issue."

"Distance is no longer an issue now that we have these new bodies," Dot said with a laugh. "I can be anywhere He calls me in moments."

"So, where in the kingdom do you two live?" Jonathan asked, "The most eastern side of the Celestial Sea, near Peter's Pier. My whole family lives on Level Path Road," Bob said.

Jonathan smiled and said, "Not to change the subject, but do you remember men's breakfast?"

"Yes, I do. Every Saturday morning, we had breakfast at my house and then we went through the book of Proverbs after we ate. It was such a blessing to host, and I had many, many fond memories of everyone who attended," Bob said.

Dot smiled brightly and said, "Our Lord has made everything perfect in its time, and our fellowship is sweeter than we could have ever imagined. I loved you and your wife, very deeply, from the heart."

"Jonathan, I remember those days well, as if they were yesterday. It's always wonderful to see young Christians grabbing ahold of the means of grace that God has given them. It's wonderful to see a life that is [123]being transformed into His likeness with that ever- increasing glory, which only comes from our Lord, who is the Spirit," Bob added.

They visited for a little while and finally parted company.

---

[123] Ephesians 2:18

They all knew they would see each other regularly, for they had all of eternity to grow in their relationship with one another. The Lord, Himself, was in the business of growing His people in love and works of service.

As Jonathan was walking, the Great Shepherd appeared at his side and began walking with him. As they walked, the Shepherd turned and smiled, saying, "I have a few people I would like you to meet, for they will be a great blessing to you. They will speak to you about hidden things and accomplish my purposes in your life. My desire is to have you grow more and more in your love for me and all the saints of the kingdom."

At once, Jonathan's heart soared; he wondered who these people might be and how these meetings were going to affect his heavenly life.

As they walked together, a man dressed in a white robe with long brown hair and a large beard was sitting on one of the white benches beside the river. As the Shepherd approached, the man stood up and walked forward.

Jonathan noticed that the man bowed down with great joy before the Lord and rose with a loving smile upon his face. His eyes seemed to shine forth with the readiness to embark on a great mission in service for the King.

"Jonathan, this is my beloved friend, Abel. He was the first martyr for the kingdom."

Jonathan's mouth dropped. He was amazed, and he was already beginning to piece together the stories he heard so many times before in the old world.

"You have heard his story throughout the ages, but now the first sacrifice of love stands before you."

The Shepherd turned to Abel and said, "Tell Jonathan your story." Abel looked at Jonathan and with great passion, he began by saying, "The Lord deserves all glory, praise and honor, and all of our attention should be on Him. Yet, He allows me to draw your gaze away from Him and His great sacrifice so that you might hear my story. How rich is His love; His kindness is without measure and His compassion is never ending. It fills me anew every morning. This is my story."

Able began, "When my parents were removed from the garden, the Lord was merciful and gave them a son. Cain was their first-born and I came after. We were raised to [124]love the Lord our God with all of our heart and with all of our soul and with all of our strength. It was my heart's delights to bring Him my first fruits, for He is the one who always blessed me and made my heart sing, for He had made my heart glad.

[125]Now, I kept flocks and Cain worked the soil. In the course of time, Cain brought some of the fruits of the soil as an offering to give to the Lord. But I brought fat portions from some of the firstborn of my flock. The Lord looked with favor on my offering, but on Cain and his offering, He did not look with favor. So, Cain became very angry, and his face was downcast.

"Now Cain said to me, 'let's go out to the field' and while we were in the field, Cain attacked me and killed me.

"Today, I stand before the saints in this white robe and the crown of life because my life became a living sacrifice, holy and pleasing to the Lord."

Jonathan then watched as Abel knelt before the Lord and took off his crown, laying it at His feet.

He then stood up and said to Jonathan, "My death was sudden and unexpected, yet I still get to tell my story, even though sin was a constant pressure and oftentimes my close companion. I am only a sinner saved by grace. I am not worthy to wear this crown, yet I do because the Lord desires for me to wear it. Many times, I have laid it down at His feet and He continually pick it up and puts it

---

[124] Deuteronomy 6:5
[125] Genesis 4:2-5, 8

back upon my head."

"He deserves all glory, praise and honor. My sacrifice was small compared to my redeemer's. [126]For I know that it was not with perishable things such as silver or gold that I was redeemed from the empty way of life handed down to me by my father, but with the precious blood of Christ, a lamb without blemish or defect."

With that final statement, Abel looked upon his Lord, his eyes shining forth the great joy that was in his heart. Jesus laid his hand on Abel's shoulder and said, [127]"Well done, good and faithful servant!"

Abel's face shined as it reflected the Lord's joy. He smiled at Jonathan and said, "I am sure we will see each other soon, my brother, and I am looking forward to hearing your testimony."

Abel walked away with great joy, and Jonathon watched him as he turned the corner down one of the streets and disappeared.

The Lord looked at Jonathan with a smile and said, "I have many other people I want you to meet, so that you may hear their testimonies unto death."

---

[126] 1 Peter 1:18-19
[127] Matthew 25-23

Chapter 12: The Son of Jehoiada

As they walked through the park, the path they were on began to rise higher and higher until they reached the summit. Looking in front of them, they could see the Great Worship Hall with its huge four angled towers rising up hundreds of feet on the four corners of the building. The massive gold dome and cupola at the center of the building rose up even higher into the clouds. To the right of them, they could see the mountain on which the majestic Throne of God stood, shining brilliantly with different shades of blue emanating from the rainbow that encircled it. They watched the River of Life flow as it began its journey from the Throne and continued down the mountain and into the distant horizon.

Jonathan breathed out slowly in awe as he was captured by the moment.

He was brought back as he heard Jesus say, "Jonathan, walk ahead a little bit farther and you will see a garden. Enter in, and you will meet one of your brothers there who gave his all for the sake of righteousness. I will see you in just a little while."

Jonathan walked a short distance and found the garden's entrance. As he walked in, he saw a man sitting on a bench dressed in white with a crown upon his head. The man got up, walked over to Jonathan and said, "Hello, Jonathan my name is Zechariah. The Lord called me here to tell you my story, and I am also looking forward to hearing yours."

Jonathan said, "I don't think my story will be as exciting as yours." Zechariah said, "We all have many stories where the Lord had become the champion in our lives. I believe [128]God's Spirit did not make you timid, but He gave you a Spirit of power, love and self-

---

[128] 2 Timothy 1:7

discipline. Jonathan, [129]God used His creative power in Christ Jesus for you to do His glorious work, which He prepared in advance for you to do. I know I will hear wonderful stories from your life, for [138]He who started a good work in you surely has brought it to completion.

"So, here is my story. I was the son of Jehoiada, the priest. I lived in the time of King Joash of Jerusalem around 800 BC. My father was a faithful priest in God's Kingdom in Judah.

"My father was a man devoted to the things of the Lord, and he even influenced [130]King Joash to do what was right in the eyes of the Lord, all the years of my father's life. He helped Joash restore the temple of the Lord, our God. As long as my father Jehoiada lived, burnt offerings were presented continually in the temple of the Lord. My father was old and full of years, and he died at the age of a hundred and thirty. He was buried with the kings in the City of David, because of the good he had done in Israel for God and His temple.

"After my father, Jehoiada, died, Joash was led astray by the officials of Judah who came, because they paid homage to him, and he listened to them. They then abandoned the temple of the Lord, the God of their fathers, and worshipped Asherah poles and idols.

"After this, God's anger came upon Judah and Jerusalem. Although the Lord sent prophets to the people testifying against the falsehood so they would return to Him, they would not listen. It was at this time that [131]the Spirit of God came upon me, and I stood before the people and said, "this is what God says: ""Why do you disobey the Lord's commands? You will not prosper. Because you have forsaken the Lord, He has forsaken you.'

---

[129] Ephesians 2:10

[130] 2 Chronicles 24:2, 15-19

[131] 2 Chronicles 24:20-22

"After this, they plotted against me, and by order of the king, they stoned me to death in the courtyard of the Lord's temple. King Joash did not remember the kindness my father Jehoiada had shown to him, but he killed me. I called out to him. My last words were, 'May the Lord see this and call you to account.'

"Today, I praise the Lord that my death was not in vain, for it encouraged many people to be faithful to the Lord, even unto death. My death was even mentioned by our Savior when he spoke to his disciples in His earthly ministry. He said in Matthew 23:34-36, 'Therefore I am sending you prophets and wise men and teachers. Some of them you will kill and crucify; others you will flog in your synagogues and pursue from town to town. And so, upon you will come all the righteous blood that has been shed on earth, from the blood of righteous Abel to the blood of Zechariah son of Berekiah, whom you murdered between the temple and the altar. I tell you the truth; all this will come upon this generation.'"

Zechariah turned and looked away from Jonathan, and he could tell that he was deep in thought. Zechariah was looking down upon the streets of gold, watching the River of Life flow. He continued to look at all the people walking, talking and enjoying the Lord's bounty.

He turned back to Jonathan and said, "Who am I that the Lord of Glory would let my story be told in light of His great sacrifice? I am mentioned in Scripture and that, in itself, is glorious enough. But now my story is being told to you today and many others also have heard it. Who am I, that the Lord of Glory would show such favor to me?"

As Zechariah finished his sentence, the Lord Jesus entered into the garden and walked over to them and said, "My beloved Zechariah, you and your father served me faithfully all the days of your life. You served my people faithfully and were a great blessing to my church throughout the ages."

"Zechariah, I have loved you before the foundations of the world were created, and I loved you when I began knitting you together in your mother's womb. I loved you as you grew up, and I directed your life like an artist controls a brush. It was always my purpose and desire to bless you all the days of your life and to bring you into my kingdom as an example of one who loved me, even unto death."

Jesus then took something from his Royal Robe, handed it to Zechariah saying, [132]"I am giving you this white stone with a new name written on it, known only to you, the one who receives it."

As Zechariah reached out and received the gift from his Savior's hands, he looked at the white stone and examined it and finally read the words that were written on it.

The words hit Zechariah deep within and filled him with an inexpressible joy. His face seemed to glow and his garments seemed even whiter, if that were possible.

The Shepherd reached out, embraced him, and said, "Welcome, my beloved friend, you were faithful with little and look now at your great reward, all this is yours, even the kingdom."

Their meeting had now ended, and as Zechariah walked home, he passed many saints and his countenance shone brightly upon them. As he passed, they smiled, for they knew he was with the Lord of Glory and something amazing must have happened.

Then, the Lord turned to Jonathan and said, "You have many more people I want you to meet." They once again began walking down into the valley below and onto the streets of gold.

---

[132] Revelation 2:17

Chapter 13: The Old Tattered Book

The Lord and Jonathan began their descent down the mountain path. To the right of them was a forest filled with what looked like pine trees that rose up hundreds of feet into the air. They were planted in perfect rows as far as the eye could see. Wildlife could be seen darting this way and that as they ran upon the needles that covered the ground. To the left of them was a steep embankment that dropped hundreds of feet down to the River of Life. They reached the bottom of the mountain and entered into a beautiful valley, known as the Valley of Delight.

The valley was filled with streams that flowed from the river. The streams entered the park on the far side of the valley and they branched out in every direction. The streams made their way back into the river on the side where Jesus and Jonathan entered. Wherever the streams entered the landscape, the vegetation flourished. Fruit trees filled the valley and different shades of the colors yellow, red and orange burst forth through the green leaves upon the trees. Many of the trees were filled with clusters of fruit causing their branches to bend and arch toward the ground."

Many people were there from all over the kingdom, for this valley was often visited by the Shepherd. It was said, "This was His garden of delight." Many people wondered what brought the Shepherd to this place so often, but one thought seemed to stand out more than any other. "Wherever the sheep are, you will find the Shepherd, or wherever the Shepherd is, you will find the sheep."

They continued walking through the valley, and as they continued, saints, angels and other heavenly hosts all bowed down as the Great Shepherd of the Kingdom passed by. They reached a spot by the river that was covered in lush green grass and white flowers. The Lord pointed to the spot under a huge fruit tree and said, "Let's sit here and finish our conversation.

"Jonathan, the kings, rulers, publicans and judges of that

sinful world refused to see the light of truth. They shut their eyes and refused to see, plugged their ears and refused to hear, hardened their hearts and refused mercy to the oppressed. They loved the praises of men rather than the praise of the God of all creation. The world was not worthy of my disciples, they killed many of them in spite of knowing the truth. They condemned the innocent and let the wicked go free. They refused to see that [133]nothing in all creation was hidden from your Heavenly Father's sight; that everything would be uncovered and laid bare before the eyes of Him to whom they must give account.

"Consider my faithful servant John, who is called the Baptist. [134]He spoke out against Herod's marriage to his brother's wife Herodias. John said, 'It was not lawful for you to have your brother's wife.' Because of this, John found himself bound and put in prison. John was a holy and righteous man, so Herod feared him and protected him, but Herodias hated John and was looking for a way to kill him. Finally, she got her wish, and Herod delivered my servant John's, head on a platter as a gift. "Consider my servant Steven, a man filled with my grace and wisdom. He did great wonders and signs before the people. The religious leaders argued with him but could not stand up to the wisdom I had given him, so they conspired against him. [135]These wicked men dragged him out of the city and stoned him. As they were stoning him, he prayed to me, "Lord Jesus, receive my spirit." And when he finally fell on his knees he cried out, 'Lord, do not hold this sin against them.' When he had finally said this, he fell asleep.

"That old world always persecuted me by persecuting my people." Jesus then stood up, reached into his royal robe and pulled out a book. He handed it to Jonathan and said, "Take this and read it."

---

[133] Mark 6:20
[134] Hebrews 4:13
[135] Acts 7:58-60

Jonathan took the book, examined it, and to his surprise he discovered it was from the old world. The book looked very old, and the pages were tattered from being read. He flipped the book over and looked at the faded title which said, FOXE'S BOOK OF MARTYRS, written by John Foxe in 1563.

Jonathan looked confused and was thinking, "Why would the Lord have him read a book from that old world."

Jesus said, "Read the first section for now, and we will talk about what you read in a little while."

At that point, Jesus left and Jonathan flipped open the book and began reading the first chapter about martyrdom.

The book gave example after example of Christians who walked the path of martyrdom. Jonathan read and discovered many different accounts of martyrs:

After the death of Stephen, a great persecution started in Jerusalem against anyone who believed Jesus was the Messiah, or a prophet. The entire church was scattered throughout Judea and Samaria, except for the apostles. Two thousand saints, including Nicanor who was one of the deacons appointed with Stephen in the book of Acts, tasted death by the hands of evil men.

When Herod Agrippa was appointed Governor of Judea, he tried to stop the spread of Christianity by attacking the leaders of the church. James the Great, the son of Zebedee, the brother of John was next to be killed by the sword. His accuser, who brought the charges against him, repented and fell down at James feet asking for forgiveness after seeing the courage and steadfastness of his confession of Christ.

He was determined that James would not receive the crown of martyrdom alone. They were both beheaded at the same time. Two other believers, named Timon and Parmenas, followed the same steps of martyrdom shortly after; one died in Philippi, and the other perished in Macedonia in 44 A.D.

Philip, who was born in Bethsaida, Galilee, was the first

to be called a disciple. He labored for the Lord in Upper Asia and suffered martyrdom by being scourged, thrown in prison and then crucified in Heliopolis, Phygia in 54 A.D.

Matthew, the tax collector from Nazareth, labored in Parthia and Ethiopia. He finished the race marked out for him in the city of Nadabah, where he was slain with a halberd spear in 60 A.D.

James the Less, the brother of Our Lord Jesus, who was elected to oversee the churches in Jerusalem was martyred at the age of ninety- four by being beaten, stoned and finally clubbed to death. He was followed by Matthias, who was elected to fill the position that Judas left, and he was stoned and then beheaded in Jerusalem.

Andrew, the brother of Peter, preached in many nations in Asia, b u t when he arrived at Edessa he was taken and crucified on a cross shaped like an "X", which became known as Saint Andrew's cross.

The people of Alexandria, before their idol, "Solemnity of Serapis", dragged Mark, who was from the tribe of Levi, till death overtook him.

Nero desired to put Peter to death, but when the church found out, they encouraged Peter to leave the city of Rome to escape Nero's clutches. As Peter was leaving through the city gate, he saw the Lord Jesus Christ and worshipped him. As Jesus was leaving, Peter asked him, "Lord, where are you going?"

He answered, "I am going again to be crucified."

Peter then realized what the Lord was asking him to do, and he returned back into the city where he was crucified. He requested that his head should be down and his feet to be up in the air, for he said, "He was unworthy to die in the same manner as the Lord Jesus Christ." The apostle Paul also suffered under the first persecution by Nero.

Nero sent two of his men, Ferega and Parthemius, to bring news of his death. They both asked Paul to pray for them that they may believe. Paul then prayed for them and encouraged them to be baptized. This done, Paul was then led away to the place of execution outside the city and he gave his neck over to the sword.

Jude, the brother of James, also called Thaddeus, was crucified at Edessa in 72 A.D.

Bartholomew preached in several countries and translated the Gospel of Matthew in India's native language. He was afterwards severely beaten and then crucified by idolaters.

Thomas, called Didymus, preached the gospel in Parthia and India where pagan priests thrust a spear through him.

Luke followed the same road as his brothers, and was hung on an olive tree in Greece by idolatrous priests.

Simon the Zealot preached the gospel in Mauritania, Africa, and even Britain where he was also crucified in the year 74 A.D.

John, the brother of James the Great, was the beloved disciple of Jesus. He founded the churches of Smyrna, Pergamum, Sardis, Philadelphia, Laodicea and Thyatira. When he was in Ephesus, he was ordered to be sent to Rome, and then he was cast into a cauldron of boiling oil. By the grace of God, he escaped without injury. Domitian afterwards exiled him to the Island of Patmos, where he wrote the book of Revelation. He was the only apostle to escape a violent death at the hands of wicked men.

Barnabas was from Cyprus and was known as the son of encouragement. He died in 73 A.D.

In spite of all the horrible persecutions and continual punishments brought by evil men, the church increased daily, rooted and established in the Apostles' teaching and watered by the blood of the saints.

As Jonathan finished reading the first section, he was deeply moved by the stories about the brothers he loved. He was joined to them and he was one of them. When they suffered, he could almost feel their pain and the stories tore at his heart. His heart was captured by the faith and enduring strength of his brothers, and his love for them increased all the more. He sat looking at the water, allowing the words to sink deep into his heart.

Jonathan turned to the next chapter and began reading.

Chapter 14: Precious in his Sight

As Jonathan turned the pages of history, he read one story after another. All the stories were precious; they all talked about the steadfast love of the martyrs and the object of their love, the Lord Jesus Christ. Some stories grabbed his attention more than others; this was only because they were written in greater detail. Jonathan knew in time that he would learn more about all their lives and all of the things they went through for the Lord's glory. One story in particular was the martyrdom of Polycarp.

Polycarp was the bishop of Smyrna in the year 162 A.D. He heard that the leaders were after him, so he made his escape, but he was discovered by a little child. After the guards who captured him finished their feasting and celebrating, he asked them if he could pray for an hour, which he was allowed. He prayed so fervently that his guards repented that they were used to capture him. He was however brought to the proconsul, where he was condemned to be burned in the market place. The proconsul said they would release him if he "Reproached Christ."

Polycarp answered them, "I have served him for eighty-six years and never once has he wronged me; how then could I ever blaspheme my King, who has saved me?"

He was then tied to a stake, but not nailed, which was their custom. He assured them that he would stand and not be moved. Upon lighting the kindling and sticks that surrounded him, the flames encircled his body like an arch and did not touch him. Upon seeing this, the executioner was ordered to pierce him with a sword. The executioner sword pierced his body and so much blood flowed from within him that it extinguished the fire. At this point, his enemies demanded that his body be consumed in the pile. After his death, his friends asked to give him a Christian burial, to which they were denied. Nevertheless, whatever remains he had left were collected, and burial was given by his friends.

In Mount Ararat in the year 108 A.D., many saints were crucified, crowned with thorns, and spears pierced their sides, imitating the Lord's crucifixion. A Roman Commander named Eustachius, who was brave and successful in his duties, was commanded by the emperor to join in an idolatrous sacrifice to celebrate his victories; but his faith in Jesus Christ was greater than his vanity. Therefore, he refused it. The ungrateful emperor was so enraged by his denial that he ordered him and his whole family to be martyred.

A few hundred years later in the year 286 A.D. a remarkable thing occurred. There was a legion of soldiers consisting of six thousand, six hundred and sixty-six men in which all of them were Christians. This legion was called the Theban Legion because the men had been from Thebias. They were stationed in the east until the emperor, Maximain, ordered them to march to Gaul to assist him against the rebels of Burgundy. They passed the Alps into Gaul under the command of Mauritius, Candidus and Exupernis and joined the empire.

Maximain ordered a general sacrifice to be made in which the whole army was to be involved. He also called his men to take an oath of allegiance and swear to assist in the extermination of the Christians in Gaul. Alarmed at these orders, each man in the Theban Legion absolutely refused to sacrifice or follow the orders that were commanded. Maximian was so enraged that he ordered the legion to be destroyed, by taking every tenth man from the rest and putting them to the sword. After the bloody execution those who remained stood steadfast in their faith. The emperor then ordered every tenth man that was alive to be put to death. This second wave of death did not shake their lives into the emperor's submission, but they continued to remain steadfast.

The officers then drew up a loyal remonstrance to the emperor, presuming this might soften the emperor's heart. The effect was the opposite; it enraged him all the more seeing their perseverance and unity. He then commanded that the whole legion should be put to death, which was immediately executed by the other troops who cut them to pieces with their swords on September 22, 286.

A man named Sebastian lived in Narbonne, Gaul in 303 A.D. He was instructed in the principle of Christianity in Milan. He then became an officer of the emperor's guard in Rome. He remained true to the Christian faith in the midst of idolatry. He did not desire or seek after the splendor that his position could take him, and he was untainted by the evil all around him. He refused to be a pagan, and the emperor ordered him to be taken to a field near the city called Campus Martius. He was then ordered to be shot to death with arrows.

Some Christians coming to the place of execution, in order to give him a proper burial, discovered signs of life in him. They then immediately moved him to a place of security and helped in his recovery. As soon as he was recovered and able to go out, he placed himself intentionally in the emperor's way as he was going to the temple. He then reprehended him for his cruelties and his unreasonable prejudices against Christianity. The emperor Diocletian was overcome with surprise for a moment, but then seized Sebastian and brought him to a place near the palace where he was beaten to death. He then ordered that his body be thrown into the sewer so that the Christians could not recover it and bury him. In spite of the order, a Christian Lady named Luciana searched for him, found him and removed him from the sewer than buried him in the catacombs.

Another story that captured Jonathan's heart was of a woman named Foelicitatis, who was an illustrious Roman Lady from a considerable family, and her virtues in Christ shined brightly, she was a devout Christian. She had seven sons whom she raised in piety. Januarius was the oldest and he was scourged and pressed to death with weights, Felix and Philip were clubbed to death, Silvanus, the fourth, was thrown from a precipice and the younger three sons, Alexander, Vitalis and Martial, were beheaded. Foelicitatis, their mother was then beheaded with the same sword a short time later.

Jonathan read account after account of his Christian brothers and sisters giving their all for Christ. He noticed that it was not only men who walked the path to martyrdom, but women, children, and whole families who were willing to give up everything, even their lives for the Great Shepherd. They laid their lives down to the flames, to the swords, to the racks and to the wild beasts. Jonathan was amazed at their character, perseverance and the love that they had for their Savior. They were willing to say they loved the Lord Jesus by writing their life's stories on the pages of history with their own blood as a lasting testimony of hearts transformed by the power of the gospel. Jonathan loved them and felt very privileged to be counted as a member of their heavenly family.

Jonathan was reminded again about the heart of fallen men; it was shocking to him to read about their wickedness. He knew the heart was desperately wicked and beyond cure, but to hear about their cruelty and their wicked decisions to slay the innocent, to trample the helpless, to torture the beloved was another eye opener to man's helpless state in the old world.

He stayed in the garden and continued to turn the pages of time as he read story after story and their testimony of blood sank deep within his heart. As he was flipping through the old book, he saw Jesus enter the garden. Jonathan looked up at his Savior and understood why they were willing to give up their lives for the Shepherd who loved them and still bore the marks of His own sacrifice.

Then Jonathan stood up and looked into his Savior's eyes, sensing that all the questions he had were about to be answered.

Jesus looked at Jonathan and said, "Yes, many of these stories you read are true, but there are many, many more that have never been told. Many of the details have been lost in human history, but not a single detail was lost or escaped your Heavenly Father's eyes. What the world has lost, thrown away and mocked, has been written down in the journals of Heaven. What the world has considered as valueless, the blood of the saints, your Heavenly Father sees as a precious gift, a jewel of great price. All those who gave up everything have not been disappointed, their righteous deeds have followed them into eternity and they are now receiving their great reward, the joy of the Lord."

As they sat, Jonathan was thinking about his own earthly life. He was considering what he had given up for the Lord in comparison to them.

Jesus then looked deep into Jonathan's eyes, and the expression on his face spoke volumes to his soul. It was a look of love and understanding, and it carried a message of assurance and acceptance and no hint of disappointment could be found.

The Lord said, "Not all my people are called to martyrdom. Jonathan, I knew your heart then, and I know it now. I know you had a desire to give me your all, and you even fantasized about what you would say to your tormentors if martyrdom did come. It was your heart's desire to show and demonstrate your love to me and prove to yourself that your faith was not in vain. I know you were terrified about being put in such a position; you loved the idea of martyrdom, yet hated and feared it at the same time. You knew, if it were up to yourself and your own strength, you would have certainly denied me, but you also knew that my Spirit was with you and you could face any challenge if I supplied you with the strength.

"You are not alone, [136]for the spirit is willing, but the body is weak. Many of my people throughout the ages dreamed great dreams of bringing glory to my name. They were looking for my approval and acceptance, but I had already done it all for them, for [137]I am the Lamb of God, who takes away the sin of the world.

"My beloved Jonathan, you were and always will be accepted, for [138]your Heavenly Father was pleased to give you the kingdom. Remember no one can add or take away from my sacrifice, for my life was given as the atoning sacrifice for your sins as well as for

---

[136] Matthew 26:41
[137] John 1:21
[138] Luke 12:32

the sins of the world, for all those who were called by my name.

"I said, [139]never will I leave you; never will I forsake you. I fulfilled that good promise to all those who were called to give their all. I was with them always; [149]when they passed through the rivers, I did not allow the waters to sweep over them. When they walked through the fire, I did not allow them to be burned and the flames did not set them ablaze. [140]Though the mountains are shaken and the hills are removed, yet my unfailing love for them was never shaken nor my covenant of peace removed, for I am the Lord, who has compassion on them."

Jonathan said to the Lord, "You have first set your love upon me, and you are the object and desire of my heart. You are what my heart longs for and my soul thirst for. You have been the song that bursts forth from my life. You fill my heart till it overflows and my soul rejoices continually, your praises are upon my lips and it is always my desire to declare them to the great congregation. How much more can I say about how I feel, for mere words cannot capture what you have done in my life."

Jesus smiled and said, "I love you too, my beloved Jonathan."

Jesus said to him, "Go and have fellowship, enjoy the [141]kingdom prepared for you before the foundation of the world and share everything I shared with you."

Jonathan walked toward his home, having even a greater awe for his brothers and sisters; to him they were like diamonds glittering on a black cloth, like the sun breaking through on a rainy dark cloudy day. He loved them and was excited at the idea of meeting all of them, for he had all of eternity in front of him to get to know them better.

Jonathan knew he would grow in his heavenly

---

[139] Hebrews 13:5
[140] Isaiah 43:2
[141] Matthew 25:34

relationships, his love, his service and his worship would keep increasing, and nothing could stop all that the Lord wanted to do in his life.

Chapter 15: From Darkness to Light

As the decades and centuries rolled by, Jonathan lost all track of time. He could not tell if he had been in the kingdom a thousand years or ten thousand years. Time was not an issue, and his heavenly body was not subject to decay because he would never grow old. He knew that the gifts God had given him would continually grow, his work would flourish and that his love would increase as God revealed more and more of Himself to him. Jonathan knew his life would be like a drink offering that was poured out, and that love would overflow to the King and the heirs of the kingdom.

One day, the Lord sent Jonathan on a journey to the far west side of the kingdom. He was going to a particular house on Straight Street where he was going to help a man named [152]Cornelius, who was hosting a banquet. He was the same Cornelius mentioned in the Book of Acts, he once lived in Caesarea where he was a centurion in the Italian regiment in the old world.

Jonathan was quite excited to meet one of the first gentiles to come to Christ. He was looking forward to hearing his story in greater detail. He finally reached Straight Street, found the house and knocked upon the door.

Jonathan heard the footsteps as they were approaching the door. As it opened, he got a good look at this famous man from biblical times. His round face beamed with joy as he reached out and grabbed Jonathan's hand and said, "O Jonathan, I heard so much about you from the Lord, I am very excited that you are here to help me serve the King of Kings and Lord of Lords at this special banquet."

He was taken aback; it was he that was excited to see him. The man who stood in front of him was led to faith by the Apostle Peter. [153]He was known in the old world as a devout and God-fearing man who was generous to those in need and he prayed to God regularly. It was amazing to Jonathan that he was even known by him.

Jonathan always considered himself just a regular Christian man who was slack in his duties, weak in prayer, had not led a single person to Christ, and never did anything really great for the Lord in his earthly life. He did not dwell on his shortcomings or sin though. He knew he could not go back and change anything, and even if he could, he would most likely be the same man that he was. He knew he was accepted in the beloved and that he was highly favored by the Lord, for the Great Shepherd loved all His sheep with an eternal and enduring love that could never be exhausted or extinguished.

Cornelius said, "Come in and make yourself at home. We have plenty of time, let's talk for a while."

As Jonathan entered the house, he noticed it had a Mediterranean design and was immediately captured by its beauty. The walls had a rough white texture with gold circular swirls for a pattern. Cornelius led Jonathan through this magnificent house with its beautiful furniture and large carved arched doorways. They walked out onto an awesome tear- drop shaped deck that overlooked a huge harbor. The deck was oval in shape and was about a hundred and fifty feet wide by a hundred feet deep. It was made out of various colored shapes of marble and onyx displaying a royal medallion seal. Off the main deck were six other smaller decks, about half the size, and they stepped down and arched their way right up to the water's edge.

Cornelius walked over to a table that had a couple of chairs set up facing the harbor and invited Jonathan to sit down with him. He then turned and said, "I love hearing stories of how our Lord has worked in the lives of his people. Tell me, how did you come to know the Lord?"

Jonathan felt like saying to him, I really want to hear your story. However, his face showed such an eagerness and determination that it forced Jonathan to look back at his own earthly life and contemplate where to begin the story.

Finally, he said, "I guess I have to start at the beginning, before I knew Christ. Then you can see how He met all my needs and filled what was lacking in my life. He has truly made it easy for me to commit my life to him. He had made the soil of my heart ready, and planted the seed of faith and love from the very beginning.

"From my teen years on, I felt a great void in my life. I knew something was missing, but I could not put my finger on it. I lived my life from one high point to the next. I said to myself, 'My life will be great and I will be happy when I finish school, when I get the perfect job, when I have a girlfriend, when I get married and all the other good things people chase after in that old world to fill the emptiness that is in their hearts. My heart was empty and I lived a life like a ship on the ocean without a compass, blown by the wind with no clear direction.

"One of the best things the Lord put in my life before I was saved was a woman named Elizabeth Manning. We were together a year or two and then we got married. I assumed at that point that she could meet all my needs and satisfy the deep longings of my heart. She was a wonderful wife, but I was still the same man I was before I got married. My life was still empty and my heart was still unsatisfied. She could not fill what the Lord left lacking.

"When I discovered that nothing had changed in my life and that the void still remained, I began to wonder if I married the wrong woman. Maybe she wasn't the one meant for me. Life didn't make sense; I loved her, but yet I still felt empty. I believed that once I was married, my life would be fulfilled and I would be satisfied. That's what I thought marriage would bring into my life.

"As you know, the problem wasn't Elizabeth, but me. I never realized that I was the problem until Christ Jesus filled what was lacking in my life. I actually expected her to meet all my needs, mend a broken heart and a crushed spirit. That's an impossible task for any wife to fi ll. "After I came to faith, she became my heart's desire. I actually grew to love her more and more as the years flew by. I delighted to be with her and wanted to spend as much time together as possible. I cherished our times alone and I loved when we would go out or get away together by ourselves. Every night when I went to bed, I held her close, or she held me and I would think to myself, I could lay here with her forever. I believe God did this for both of us, he made our marriage blossom and kept out the sin that could have so easily entangled it."

Cornelius asked, "Is Elizabeth here, and is she one of the redeemed?" Jonathan's face lit right up as he said, "She is here, and I am near her always. God did not break up our marriage, but He fulfilled it. God has made our relationship even better and more fulfilling; we are much more than husband and wife. God did not take her out of my life, for in His perfect wisdom, He has completed the union He had joined together. I still love her, my children and all those that were close to my heart, very deeply. Our relationship continues to grow and develop, for God did not destroy marriage but gave us something even better, eternity with the ones we love.

"I had two children in the old world, a boy named Ben and a girl named Sarah. They are here also, and it's a joy to spend time with them. Praise God He didn't take those we loved and separated us from them, but instead He made those same relationships blossom even brighter."

"I can't wait to meet...." Cornelius' words were interrupted by some voices behind them. As they turned, Jonathan saw his earthly family walk through the arched doorway.

Jonathan turned to Cornelius and said, "You are about to meet my family now."

Cornelius stood up and invited them to sit down with them and said, "Welcome, it is amazing how our God can answer the prayers that are still upon our lips. I was just telling Jonathan that I could not wait to meet you and now here you are."

After everyone introduced themselves, Elizabeth was moved to read a Psalm. [142] After the Psalm was read, someone started

---

[142] Ephesians 5:19-20

singing a hymn, and then another spiritual song followed. They found themselves singing and making music in their hearts to the Lord.

After they were finished singing, Jonathan said, "Cornelius wanted to hear my testimony, and I was just at the beginning of it."

He then turned to Cornelius and said, "Would you like me to finish it now?"

Cornelius said with an excited smile, "Yes, let's continue."

Jonathan turned to his family, "You have heard my testimony about a thousand times, are you sure you want to sit through it again?"

All three of them said, "No," simultaneously and everyone laughed. Cornelius said to the others, "Why don't you get things ready and Jonathan can finish his story." They all agreed and went to wherever their duties called them.

Jonathan knew he would tell the same story many more times as he met new brothers and sisters. He would never get sick of telling his story, and he would never get sick of hearing their stories either. Another reason Jonathan loved the stories is that the Lord, Himself, often appeared during these meetings to uncover deep hidden truths in the heart and souls of men. He would show how His hand was in the midst, wooing the beloved to His side. He knew his testimony was not given to evangelize, but to give praise, glory and honor to the King of Kings and Lord of Lords.

Jonathan continued, "I was brought up in a church where God's Word was read in a limited manner, but many people were saved. I always believed myself to be a Christian because of my upbringing. I had a limited knowledge of God though, and an impersonal relationship with Jesus Christ; I didn't know him as my Lord and Savior.

"I also lived my life in such a way that I had no desire for the things of God, and the things of that old world filled my life. I was a Christian in name only; my heart, mind and soul belonged to the world and I lived in it, unsatisfied.

"I had my brother, named Andrew, who was living with me when I first got married; he was and is a believer. We would often have talks about Jesus, and then I would get frustrated for one reason or another and these talks would end in arguments. He would often invite me to his church, but I would never go. One day, I finally decided to go, maybe because he wore me down by asking so many times. I am so glad now that he kept on inviting me persistently.

"The church that he brought me to was so small, in fact, they were meeting in a house; it was totally different from what I grew up with. They had a Bible on every seat, and the people sang with joy. Even after the message, the people did not rush out, but stayed and visited with each other.

"As I think of it now, their meetings were like those mentioned in the Scriptures, in the Book of Acts, which says; [143]"They devoted themselves to the Apostles' teachings and to the fellowship, to the breaking of bread and to prayer. All the believers were together and had everything in common. They broke bread in their homes and ate together with glad and sincere hearts, praising God and enjoying the favor of all the people.'

"Little did I know that the Lord would be adding me to their number the following week, and here is how it happened. "I attended my brother's church, and the minister asked if he could come over for a visit. We set a date and time for a meal the following week; a night of drinking, socializing and having fun, or so I thought.

"We did enjoy our meal and conversations, but as the night moved on, the minister changed the direction of how the night was progressing. He did this by asking me a question that would change my life forever.

---

[143] Acts 2:42-47

"He asked, 'Jonathan, if your wife Elizabeth sent you on an errand and on the way, you died in an accident and God was to ask you, 'Why should I let you into my kingdom?' How would you answer him? For the Bible says, [144]"Man is destined to die once, and after that to face judgment, [145]for we must all appear before the Judgment Seat of Christ, so that each one may receive what is due him for the things done while in the body, whether good or bad.'

"So Jonathan, how would you answer the one who sits on a Great White Throne, the one that makes [146]earth and sky flee from His presence, and there is no place for them? So how would you answer His question, 'Why should I let you into my kingdom?'

"I answered the way the rest of mankind answers, those who do not know the righteousness that comes from God. I answered, 'I hope that God would overlook my sin and that He would see that I am not all that bad compared to many other people. I think if you were to weigh my good deeds and bad deeds on a scale, the good deeds would out-weigh the bad. I don't think I ever really did anything bad enough to deserve Hell. I never killed anyone, never stole anything of real value, and I am not out to hurt people. All in all, I'm not that bad of a guy. I also suffered enough in this world. I guess I just hope God would overlook my faults.'

"'So, Jonathan, you would say you are an average guy, not evil and not overly good?'

"'I agree.'

"'Let's see how God would evaluate your answer.'

"He then read Romans 3, 'There is no one righteous, not even one; there is no one who understands, no one who seeks God. All have turned away, and have together become worthless; there is

---

[144] Hebrews 9:27
[145] 2 Corinthians 5:10
[146] Revelation 20:11

no one who does good, not even one. Their throats are like open graves; their tongues practice deceit. The poison of vipers is on their lips and their mouths are full of cursing and bitterness. Their feet are swift to shed blood; ruin and misery mark their ways, and the way of peace they do not know. There is no fear of God before their eyes.'

"'So, Jonathan, if you were going to die today, would God welcome you into His kingdom with open arms because you are such a good person?'

"I said, 'No!'

"Jonathan, I hate to say it, but you are even worse than you think you are, and you are in a terrible position. The good news is that God loves you and me. He uses very hard words that hurt our pride, but He does this to get our attention. He wants us to see our need for Him, so He uses those hard words to convict you and me of our sin and silence any debate that we may have with Him regarding our right to His kingdom, because of our righteousness.

"God doesn't want a debate, [147]He wants every mouth to be silenced and the whole world held accountable to Him, because no one can be declared righteous in His sight by observing the law, by being good.

"Here is your predicament: it's like you are in a small boat, heading for the falls without a paddle and if you go over those falls you will die. In the same way, if you stood before God's judgment seat tonight you would die. Your sin would immediately separate you from God's presence and you would go where you don't want to go. Your sin would cast you into Hell, where there will be [160]weeping and gnashing of teeth and where the worm does not die.

"Jonathan, you are heading toward the falls and the current of the way you live is too strong to paddle against it. There are steep walls of sin that are closing you in and you don't have the ability to save yourself.'

---

[147] Romans 3:19-20

"The minister hammered the final nail into the coffin when he said, 'The scriptures declare that the wages of sin is death, and your sins collect a penalty, that penalty is death. God has every right to exclude you from His kingdom because of your sin. What kind of God would overlook sin? He would not be holy. But we know God is holy and just and that your sin has to be dealt with.

"My final question is this, 'Do you want a lifeline? Do you want salvation from certain doom? Do you want to hear good news?'"

Just as Jonathan finished his sentence, something caught his eye on the other side of the bay. A small cloud appeared and seemed to be growing larger and larger as it traveled across the bay towards them. The cloud began to change its shape into a funnel, and as it moved, it began lapping up the water from the bay. It continued to grow higher and higher and spin faster and faster. Then, fire began to appear in the midst of the whirlwind and it continued to increase until the wind, the water and the fire blended together in perfect unity as it crossed the bay.

It finally stopped in front of Cornelius's house and it rose up hundreds of feet in the air. The sight brought Jonathan and Cornelius to their feet and they didn't even notice Elizabeth, William and Sarah standing at their sides. Suddenly, a voice came from the whirlwind and said, [148]"This is my beloved Son, whom I love; with Him I am well- pleased. Listen to Him!"

The whirlwind suddenly stopped, and the water that was in the midst of the whirlwind began to fall back into the bay from hundreds of feet in the air, and a light mist of water fell upon their faces. The fire that was in the whirlwind remained for a moment, and as they watched, it rose higher and higher into the heavens until finally it disappeared. As they lowered their heads, they saw Jesus walking upon the water towards them.

---

[148] Matthew 17:5

The Lord Himself stood before them and [149]His face shone like the sun, and His clothes became as white as the lightning. At that point, everyone felt that the testimony could wait, and they fell before Him. Words seemed to enter into the deep recesses of Elizabeth's heart and she prayed out loud these words of worship:

"Oh Lord, our God, You are awesome in splendor and majesty. You are the Great Shepherd and we love to hear your voice, it is so pleasant upon our ears, our eyes are always looking toward you, for you are captivating in every way. Your presence makes our hearts overflow with love that cannot be contained and measured. That love fills our lives and it overflows into the entire kingdom. You, and you alone, are the Wellspring of Life and we are yours and you are ours, our Great Reward."

The Lord opened up His arms and embraced them all and said, "You are my beloved, wherever you are, I will be. For, I am the Bridegroom and you are the bride. We have an eternal union that is bound with cords of love to the blood of the Covenant that justified and sanctified you. You will always be our heart's delight and our treasured possessions; each and every one of you has been created for eternal life. Though fathers and mothers would forsake their children in the old world, you will never be forsaken; for I have engraved your names upon the palms of my hands as an eternal promise of my everlasting love that will always pour out upon you."

"I have come to speak into Jonathan's conversion and to enjoy the banquet that you are preparing in our honor. I am looking forward to this special time together, and now let me show each of you the Spirit's power that works in the hearts of men."

---

[149] Matthew 17:2

Chapter 16: The Spirit's Power

Then Jesus said, "To begin with, salvation was a miracle of the heart. There are so many things that blinded the natural man from seeing his need   for salvation. There was a huge wall that no man could ever climb, which separated him from having a relationship with God, his Creator. There were many huge stones in the wall that caused the separation between God and man, but let's consider one for now, the human heart.

[150]"The human heart was deceitful above all things and beyond cure. Who could understand it? It was desperately wicked and every inclination of it was evil from childhood. It was not always that way. In the garden it was not evil or hard, but it was tender, loving and good. But Adam's sin pulled the heart down to lowly places, to the grave and death. As the child grows into a man, oftentimes the heart grows harder and harder until it becomes like stone. This is indeed a mystery that we will discuss later.

"Jonathan, you could not come to me because of the wall you built around your heart, and that wall had to be removed so a new heart could be given. My Spirit gently toiled and labored and penetrated the strongholds of your heart on that special day. The heart that was there was sick with death and beyond cure, so [164]we gave you a new heart and put a new spirit within you. We removed your heart of stone and gave you a heart of flesh; one that would grow to be tender, loving, good and upright.

"When you heard the words, 'There is no one righteous, not even one,' my Spirit spoke to your heart and you knew it was true. You knew with certainty that you had fallen short of all my glory and commands. I wanted you to know how much you sinned and turned away from me and the loving kindness of your heavenly Father. I wanted you to know that you lived a life that did not satisfy me or my

---

[150] Jeremiah 17:9

Father. "As you now know, I did this to draw you to me, not to drive you away. I wanted you to see the depths of your sin, so that you would see that I was your greatest need. For I have loved you with an everlasting love, and have drawn you with cords of loving-kindness. My intention was always to draw you to my side and make you my child and to be my beloved friend. I made known to you the Path of Life and I opened the gate so that you could enter into my Father's fold, into a relationship that can never perish, spoil or fade. My heart's desire was that you would understand the relationship I wanted to have with you.

"Remember my words, [151]'I no longer call you servants, because a servant does not know his master's business.' Instead, I have called you friends, for everything that I learned from my Father, I have made known to you."

Then the Lord looked into Jonathan's eyes and said, "You were, and always will be, my child and friend. Please continue on with your testimony. I will listen and shine the light on the hidden things that you never knew took place on that day."

Jonathan said with a smile and a look of hope, "Lord, it would be much more interesting and exciting if you just finished my story."

Jesus smiled and said,

"Continue on, Jonathan."

Jonathan continued his story with great joy, not with fear or anxiety of possibly saying the wrong thing. He was confident that the Lord would be pleased with his testimony, and that the Lord's love would fill his heart. He was also waiting with great expectations for Him to reveal the mysteries regarding his salvation.

Jonathan said, "At that point, the minister asked if I would like some good news, news that would bring great joy to my heart, soul and mind.

"I said, 'Yes, I want good news. Please tell me anything

---

[151] John 15:5

that can fix the situation that I am now in.'

"I didn't know, at that moment, that the words the minister was about to say would change my life forever. The man I was would slowly disappear and I would begin a new life and wonderful journey into the kingdom of God.

"So, here's what the minister said, 'I have good news for you, but it is more than that; it is great news. God has intervened on your behalf and made a way out of your predicament for you. This great news has been proclaimed to the whole world. Let me begin by saying your sin problem began even before you were born. It started at the beginning of creation.'

"Remember the story in the Bible about Adam and Eve and how they were deceived by the serpent? The Lord said, [152]'You are free to eat from any tree in the garden, but you mustn't eat from the tree of the knowledge of good and evil, for when you eat of it you will surely die.' As you know, they did eat from the tree. Then they were removed from the garden and eventually they died.

"The minister then turned to another passage and he read it to me saying, [153]'Therefore, just as sin entered the world through one man (Adam), and death came through sin, and in this way death came to all men because all have sinned.

"'You see Jonathan, we are all from the same mold, and we all have the same imprint of Adam stamped upon our lives. All mankind has walked in his footsteps of disobedience to God's commands, and if we continue to walk in that path, the hands of death will certainly grab ahold of us and bring us to the place we don't want to go.'

"The minister said with great passion, 'Now the good news, God has provided a solution for the sinner's problem, which is found in the Lord Jesus Christ. He is the perfect remedy for our sin because He is fully God and fully man. He is the perfect solution to

---

[152] Genesis 2:15-17
[153] Romans 5:12

our problem, for He can hold God's hand and man's hand at the same time.

""This is a profound mystery, but it is declared throughout the Scriptures. Let's turn to a few passages that will explain what I'm saying in greater detail.'

"The minister turned to the Scriptures that day and I hung on every word that he said."

At this point Jesus spoke up and said, "Let me show you the Scriptures that you turned to that day."

Even as He began to speak, they hung on his every word. [169]Their hearts burned in them as He opened up the Scriptures to them."

"Jonathan, on the day of your salvation, it was I who moved in you by my Spirit and I breathed life into you. I made the soil of your heart tender, so that [154]my words, which the minister used, would go out and not return to me empty, but that they would accomplish everything I desired, and achieve the purpose for which I sent it.

"I made known to you on that day that [155]my origins were of old, from ancient times, and I wanted you to know the [156]glory that I had before the creation of the world because the Father loves me. I declared to you that I was the one [157]who created everything, the things in heaven and on earth, the visible and the invisible, all powers, rulers, authorities and thrones were created by me and for me. I was before all these things, and in me all these things are held together. I am the head of the church; I am the beginning and the firstborn from among the dead, so that in everything, I will have supremacy. My intention was to save you, Jonathan, and to save you completely. I proclaimed to your heart that

---

[154] Isaiah 55:11
[155] Micah 5:2
[156] John 17:24
[157] Colossians 1:15-18

I was your perfect salvation, your perfect redeemer, who is fully God and fully man.

"As the Scriptures say, '[158]The virgin will have a child and she will give birth to a son, and they will call him Immanuel'—which means, 'God with us,' and [159]His name will be Jesus, because He will save His people from their sins.' "I then brought you to the foot of my cross, where mercy and justice meet. I am the sinless, Holy One, and I took the sins of the world upon myself."

Jesus looked into Jonathan's eyes and said, "I showed you my righteousness and my redemption at [160]just the right time; when you were still powerless, I died for the ungodly. Very rarely will anyone die for a righteous man, though for a good man someone might possibly dare to die. But I demonstrated my own love for you in this: while you were still a sinner, I died for you to bring you to God.

"I showed you the very depths of my love, for [161]I am the Lamb of God who takes away the sin of the world. Today I still bear the marks of judgment, and the empty grave testifies to my victory over sin. "Today you are all wearing white robes which declare my perfect righteousness and eternal salvation. I used tender words to draw and call all of you. Now, share with each other the words that made the biggest impact upon your lives."

Upon saying this, Jesus left Jonathan, Cornelius and the others.

As they considered His words, Elizabeth spoke first and said, "I was lonely and afflicted and I lacked the love that my heart truly desired. I remember the day the Lord drew me with his unfailing love; these are the words I heard: [178]"come to me, all you who are

---

[158] Matthew 1:23
[159] Matthew 1:21
[160] Romans 5:6-8
[161] John 1:29

weary and burdened, and I will give you rest. Take my yoke upon you and learn from me, because I am gentle and humble in heart, and you will find rest for your souls. For my yoke is easy to bear, and my burden is light.' "I was weary and burdened, for I desired love. I was in constant turmoil and my soul was downcast and desired rest. I wanted to come to the Lord to find the rest He promised, but I was afraid of rejection. I felt that this promise was for others, for those that were worthy. I was worried that if my own husband did not love me the way he should, how then could God ever love me?

"At that time, I was beginning to read the Scriptures and I came upon a verse that gave me real hope. This verse spoke to my heart; suddenly I had confidence that I would receive all the love that God promised me."

[162]"All that the Father gives me will come to me, and whoever comes to me I will never drive away."

Suddenly, the Spirit was upon Elizabeth who proclaimed, "The Lord is my strength, my redeemer and my faithful husband, the keeper of my soul. My soul delights in the Lord; He is my shield, my High Tower and my Shelter from the storm. He looked down on my lowly position, lifted me from the ash heap and put my feet on solid ground.

[163] "He gave me a crown of beauty instead of ashes, the oil of gladness instead of mourning, and a garment of praise instead of a spirit of despair. I have become like an oak of righteousness, a planting of the Lord for the display of His splendor. I delight greatly in the Lord; my soul rejoices in my God."

Elizabeth concluded with great joy and praise by saying, [164]"For He has clothed me with garments of salvation and arrayed me in a robe of righteousness."

Everyone joined in sharing their own testimonies, and when they had finished, Cornelius closed the conversation with these

---

[162] John 6:37
[163] Isaiah 61:3
[164] Isaiah 61:10

words.

"Consider this, my brothers and sisters. We are able to share our testimonies with each other, but we are also able to share our lives with each other, to love each other from the heart. We will be able to tell others how God delivered us when we were crushed in spirit, and how He ministered to us when our lives were ebbing away.

"We will hear stories after stories from our brethren who lived throughout the ages. We will hear stories about great revivals and days of great persecution. We will hear stories of heroes of the faith and martyrs, and we will be able to see how our God has always rescued His people from the hands of His enemies.

"We have all of eternity to hear about [165]Gideon, Barak, Samson, Jephthah, David, Samuel and the prophets. We will hear how through faith they toppled kingdoms, made justice work and believed in God's promises. Many, as you know, were protected from lions, fires and sword. How many stories will we hear of people who turned disadvantage to advantage, won battles and routed foreign armies? We will hear of how many women received their loved ones back from the dead. There were those who we don't know who, when under torture refused to give in and be free, preferring something better in the resurrection of the dead. Many of our brothers and sisters will tell us how they braved abuse and whips, chains and dungeons. We hear stories of those who were stoned, sawed in two, murdered in cold blood; stories of vagrants wandering the earth in animal skins, homeless, friendless, powerless—the world didn't deserve them!

"I now realize that we have all the time in eternity to meet the brethren and we know that it will be in God's perfect timing when these meetings will take place. We also know that the Lord will speak into the testimonies of these people for [166]He reveals deep

---

[165] Hebrews 11:32-39
[166] Daniel 2:22

and hidden things; He knows what lies in darkness, for light dwells with Him.

As they considered these things, they knew that their God, not man, would receive all the glory due His name.

After their discussions, many others joined Jonathan, Cornelius and their families to get ready for the banquet. On all the decks they began to lay out beautiful blue rugs that had a gold leaf pattern for their borders. Next came the couches, tables and chairs, which were arranged in perfect position so that intimate fellowship could take place by everyone who attended. After this, the decorations came, various colored drapes blew in the wind as they hung on weaved golden ropes that were attached to bronze posts on the corners of each deck. Next, the flowers and plants came, and they were placed in perfect positions to dress the remaining areas. Finally, the food and drinks came; a royal feast was laid out for the King of Kings.

Jonathan and his family left before the banquet began, but as they were leaving, they saw many familiar faces, most of them from Cornelius's generation. Many of the original deacons mentioned in the Book of Acts attended, as well as a jailer from the Old World with his family and friends. Many of the early disciples were there, from Barnabas the great encourager to Timothy with his mother, Eunice, and his grandmother Lois.

Jonathan and his family took the long way home and had wonderful discussions along the way. It was a great day and they knew that many, many more would follow.

Chapter 17: The Books Were Opened

As years rolled on, Jonathan enjoyed all the blessings and pleasures his eternal home offered. Boredom was a thing of the past, something that disappeared a long, long time ago in a world that did not even exist anymore. The Lord of the Kingdom gave abundant life to everyone, so their lives were always fruitful and enjoyable. There was always something to do, something new to see, someone to visit, some job that needed completion. Worship was continual, [167]for everything that was done, was done for the glory of God. The heirs of the kingdom could say with great confidence that their King satisfied them every morning with his unfailing love. They continually sang for joy, and they knew they would be glad all their days. Jonathan smiled and thought, [168]"He has truly made everything new."

One day Jonathan walked over to his dear friend Robert Smith's house, a man who was his pastor in the old world. They visited often and had lots of enjoyment from each other's company. They talked about many things, things they were involved in in the kingdom and things in the old world. They enjoyed seeing how the Lord had directed their steps in both places. Jonathan always loved Robert, but now their relationship grew even stronger, and it continued to grow and grow with leaps and bounds.

After he arrived at Robert's house, the two men sat down in the living room and were enjoying each other's company. Jonathan said to Robert, "It is wonderful how everything is made perfect here. The Lord left no detail unnoticed, even our homes are made to fi t our heavenly lives perfectly. We have everything we need to serve the Lord and the rest of the heirs of the kingdom without all those earthly limitations and entanglements."

Robert added, "Know what else is amazing? It's where

---

[167] 1 Corinthians 10:31
[168] Revelation 21:5

He has placed all our homes. They are in close proximity to all those we loved and cherished in the old world. It's truly a blessing to see people we loved but didn't expect to see here in the Kingdom, enjoying all that God had prepared for them. I've learned that God's mercy extended way past what we expected and His salvation reached so much farther than I have ever imagined."

Jonathan added, "It reminds me of what a Godly man said after the death of a family member. He said, 'God's grace may go out farther than we expect, the tent pegs of His grace may reach out farther than where we would have put them. When we see the death of our loved ones, we must entrust their souls into our Heavenly Father's hands. His hands are engraved with mercy and compassion and He will do what is just and upright. We can trust Him and commit our loved ones into His hands.

Robert said "Many of us had made salvation so hard, every 't' had to be crossed and every 'i' dotted, but the Lord said, [186]everyone who calls on the name of the Lord will be saved."

"That is so true. His grace also reaches much further than I had ever expected. It is a wonderful thing to be a part of the kingdom, even though many others that we loved were rejected and found themselves under the Lord's condemnation. It was such a sad, sad state, for many [187]rejected the grace that could have been theirs in Christ Jesus."

There was silence for a moment as they considered the implications of this last statement. Then Jonathan asked Robert,

"What are some of the things that captured your attention most of all at the Final Judgment?"

There was a pause for a moment as Robert began collecting his thoughts. Finally, he responded, "The sheer magnitude of it. There were so many people, millions upon millions upon millions. It was so amazing to see so many people from every generation, culture and every country; to see all of humanity there, from every man that was rich to every man that was poor, the young and the old, sea captains to farmers, from the false prophets, to those who preached a false gospel. It was such a vast crowd; it was so huge. The crowd stretched from horizon to horizon, as far as the eye could see.

"I never realized how many people dwelt upon the earth. The whole process will always be written on my mind. I see the truth in the Scripture that says, [169]"We all must appear before the Judgment Seat of Christ." I am so glad that day is over, even though we were victorious and we were accepted in the beloved. They had so many people that were broken and their hearts and souls lay bare under the weight of their sin."

Robert said softly, "I also remember on that day, no one lifted their head in pride or arrogance but everyone was brought low, very low. We also were sinners like them who entered into eternal shame, but by the grace of God we could stand because [189]our advocate never left our side." Jonathan nodded in agreement.

Robert continued, "It was a sad day for them, but for us it was a day of victory and reconciliation. Our hearts and souls were lifted because the Lord was our advocate on that day, for He had supplied His loved ones with His eternal righteousness."

Jonathan said, "There is truly only [190]one mediator between God and man, and He is Christ Jesus the Lord."

As they were still speaking, a bright light appeared in the midst of them. It grew in intensity until the Glory of the Lord totally engulfed them. Seconds later they found themselves transported to the Great Hall of Worship. All over the hall, millions and millions of saints, angels and other heavenly beings began to appear.

The Great King was seated at the front of the assembly and the Lord Jesus was at His right hand. Jesus was looking out over the vast crowd, and when everyone was there and settled in place, He stood up. As He stood, the train of His royal robe began to flow down

---

[169] 2 Corinthians 5:10

the stairs of the throne and onto the sea of glass. He then raised His hands high and the sleeves of His robe slipped down so that the traces of His wounds could be seen by the multitudes, and He said to them with a voice that sounded like a gentle wind blowing through the trees on a sunny day, [170]"Blessed are you who were poor in spirit, for you have received the Kingdom of Heaven. Blessed are you who mourned, for you have now been comforted. Blessed are you who were meek, for you have now inherited the new Heaven and the new Earth. Blessed are you who hungered and thirsted for righteousness, for you have now been filled. Blessed are you who were merciful, for you have now been shown great mercy. Blessed are you who were pure in heart, for you have now seen God. Blessed are you who were peacemakers, for you have now been called the children of God. Blessed are you who were persecuted because of righteousness, for you are now in the Kingdom of Heaven. Blessed were you when people insulted you, persecuted you, and falsely said all kinds of evil about you because of me, for look around, rejoice and be glad, because great is your reward here in the kingdom."

The Great Shepherd sat back down upon His throne at the right hand of the Father. A moment later, a light mist of water and a gentle flame appeared, and it seemed to rise up from the Father and the Son. Jonathan noticed that the mist of water and flame began to increase in size until it encompassed the entire throne. It continued to increase until the entire sea of glass before the throne was also covered. Jonathan also noticed that he could still see very clearly through the mist of water and fire to the throne. The mist of water and fire began to roll outward like a deep fog and it began to engulf the heavenly host. The Spirit began working in the hearts of the people as it slowly rolled over them, and wherever the mist of water and fire was, the praise started. It continued to grow until the mist of water and the fire permeated every part of the great assembly, which

---

[170] Matthew 5:3-10

moved all the people to praise the God of Heaven in perfect unity and in one accord.

The worship was beyond any earthly description. Jonathan's worship did not have to be forced, and he did not have to drum up or manipulate his feelings. His heart was free and complete, fully made for praise. His heart felt as if it would burst wide open if he remained silent. So he lifted his hands high and his voice proclaimed the joy that flowed from his heart. He cried out in complete unison with the heavenly host.

The worship continued, and many things were said and done that filled the hearts of the saints with praise and great expectations for future events. Jonathan was continually surprised at how the Lord could fill all his days with new joys in worship. So this day, like all the other days, he [171]worshiped in Spirit and in Truth, for that is the type of worshippers the Father seeks, for God is Spirit and His worshipers must worship him in the Spirit and truth.

The time of corporate worship came to an end, and the Lord dismissed them.

As Jonathan was leaving, Robert came to Jonathan's side and said, "Are you free to finish our conversation, or do you have duties that need attending? Before Jonathan could answer, a mighty hand fell upon both their shoulders. To their surprise, they turned and saw Moses, whom they had often seen but never talked to.

Moses was smiling and said, "The Lord told me about your conversations regarding the final judgment and thought it would be even more interesting for you if I was there." A broader smile filled Moses' face and he added, "It would not surprise me if the Lord, Himself, and many others might join us in this interesting conversation."

---

[171] John 4:23-24

115

Chapter 18: Moses' Judgment

They all left together with great smiles upon their radiant faces. They were all looking forward to hearing about each other's perspectives of the final judgment and they wondered what the Lord would reveal to them about the subject.

As they left the massive hall, they walked toward the great mountains in the east. They could see their peaks as some of the clouds parted. They were huge mountains, which many of the saints climbed to get a better look at the size of the great kingdom, but still only a fraction of it could be seen. It was going to be an interesting visit Jonathan thought, as he walked down the streets of gold with his good friend, Robert, and the Old Testament patriarch, Moses.

They walked through the city streets, and they were pointing here and there at all the beauty around them. They continued down the streets of the city and found a little alcove, which they could use for their discussions.

The alcove was about thirty feet wide and sixty feet long, and the walls on each side were made out of wood with inlays of pure gold and pictures of pomegranates and cherubim. The brightness of the Lord shone in and it illuminated the place, for the [172]heavenly city did not need the sun or the moon to shine on it for the glory of the Lord gave the city its light.

They entered in and sat down on benches that were decorated with engravings of the River of Life. Each leg of the benches was carved in great detail to resemble trees with fruit and flowers budding. The seats that were there were set up in such a way, as if a meeting was meant to be taken place right there. They even had a table laid out with various breads, fruits and juices. As they looked around, the excitement began to build in their hearts, and they all knew great conversations awaited them.

---

[172] Revelation 21:23

Moses was the first to reach out for the bread. He passed it around to the others and they poured their own drinks. Moses was the first to begin to speak, "It looks like the Lord has [173]prepared a table before us and our cups overflow. Surely His goodness and love will follow us all our days." They all agreed. Giving thanks, they began to eat.

While they were eating, Moses began the conversation by speaking first to Robert, "The Lord told me that you both remembered the magnitude, the sheer size of the final judgment and the vast numbers of people that stood before the Throne, but what else stands out in your memories?"

Robert let the question roll around in his mind for a bit and finally answered, "A few things, it was amazing who was judged and how they were judged."

"Start with whom, and then why. What about these things impressed you?" Moses instructed.

"To begin with, I remembered Jesus' words regarding judging generations, and I never really thought about it until that day. It was amazing to see how His words came to fulfillment and how everything played out.

"I never thought about how the words of Jesus would fully play out when He said that the [174]Queen of the South will rise at the judgment and condemn the men of that generation and that the men of Nineveh will stand up at the judgment with that generation and condemn it.

"I will always remember the part of the judgment when the Pharisees and Sadducees were brought to the throne of God as a group. It was so amazing to see all of them there and all the others that stood opposed to Jesus. To see that generation standing before the judgment seat, and having them see the Lord Jesus at the Father's right side dressed in royal splendor was incredible."

Moses added, "I will always remember that day, for they

---

[173] Psalm 23:5-6
[174] Luke 11:29-32

actually, and foolishly, [175]set their hopes on me, as if I am somebody who could save them. They studied my words, but they missed the whole meaning. [176]They pursued a law of righteousness and tried to receive God's favor by works instead of by faith. [177]They stumbled over the stumbling stone. That Law, which the Lord gave me, which was engraved in stone, was put in place to lead them to Jesus Christ. They misused that Law and it became a stumbling stone and the rock that made them fall."

Moses shook his head in remembrance and continued, "I remember watching Jesus' earthly ministry from Heaven, and I watched how they treated my Lord. I remember watching the events unfold, hearing the harsh words that were said about Him, and seeing the evil plans that they were putting together. It was so hard to see the Lord go through such opposition. We watched His rejection by the people, His betrayal, His great suffering in the garden, and seeing them [178]spit in His face and strike Him with their fists and seeing others slap Him and say, 'Prophesy to us, Christ. Who hit you?' We had seen it all, and our hearts were broken."

Robert added, "I remember when their earthly words and deeds came back upon them and how the words they said echoed throughout the great assembly. I still shiver just thinking about Jesus' words when He said of them, [179]'Anyone who speaks a word against the Son of Man will be forgiven, but anyone who speaks against the Holy Spirit will not be forgiven, either in this age or in the age to come.'"

Jonathan jumped in and added, "I remember now, that generation received much more condemnation then other generations because they were given so much more. Where much is given; much

---

[175] John 5:45
[176] Romans 9:32
[177] Galatians 3:24
[178] Matthew 26:67
[179] Matthew 12:32

is demanded."

Robert continued, "One amazing event was when the Queen of Sheba was brought forth and the place was shaken by her accusations that condemned that generation."

As Robert was still speaking, a woman entered the alcove and everyone looked up as she entered. Their eyes went wide and smiled as the Queen of Sheba, herself, entered and greeted them.

Chapter 19: The Queen's Judgment

The Lord told me about your conversation and He sent me here to talk with you. You must be just beginning to talk about my testimony at the final judgment." They all welcomed her in and introduced themselves.

Moses said, "I am so glad you are here. I have been waiting for an opportunity to speak to you since the day I first heard your testimony, and now the Lord has opened that door. Please tell us what the Lord has put on your heart." The rest of them nodded in agreement.

[180] "To begin with, my name is Saba, I was a queen in a distant land and I heard about Solomon's fame and his relationship with the Lord. I traveled a great distance to test him with many hard questions. I met with King Solomon and he answered all of my questions; nothing was too hard for him to explain to me. When I saw all the wisdom Solomon had and the palace he had built, all the food on his table, the seating of his officials, and his servants in their robes, his cupbearers and the burnt offerings he made at the temple of the Lord, I was totally overwhelmed."

"I said to King Solomon, 'The report I heard in my own country about your achievements and your wisdom is true.' But I did not believe these things until I came and saw it with my own eyes. Indeed, not even half was told to me; in wisdom and wealth you have far exceeded the report I have heard. How happy your men must be! How happy your officials, who continually stand before you and hear your wisdom! Praise be to the Lord your God, who has delighted in you and placed you on the throne of Israel. Because of the Lord's eternal love for Israel, He has made you King, to maintain justice and righteousness. "So, I met with Solomon, the King of Israel, when I

---

[180] 1 Kings 10:1-9

sojourned on the earth. I traveled a great distance to meet Solomon and I was satisfied. My Lord, the King of Heaven and Earth traveled a great distance also. He traveled from His Eternal Throne to be a babe in a manger, from His heavenly kingdom to earth's lowest regions. My Lord traveled so much farther than I ever did, for He humbled Himself of His kingly authority and became a man. As you know from the scriptures and my testimony, I was called forth as a witness at the Final Judgment against that generation.

"You may not know this, but Jesus' own words burned in my heart on that day. I could not be silent, so I echoed His words as a testimony against them. I remembered saying to them, [181]'I traveled many, many miles to hear Solomon's wisdom and was completely satisfied from what I saw and heard.' I knew that he was a man that God had blessed and that he had a relationship with the Great God of Israel, who is the God of all nations. I was very impressed with his wisdom and knowledge, and nothing was too hard for him. I received one blessing after another as he revealed many mysteries to me. No question was too hard for him. Solomon though was just a man, a man filled with wisdom, and his kingdom was filled with splendor.

[182]"'I traveled from the ends of the earth to listen to Solomon's great wisdom, and one greater than Solomon was there in your time.

"'I came to Solomon, who is only a man, but God came to you and you closed your eyes to the splendor of his coming. You closed your hearts to the words of eternal life and you closed the door to the invitation for reconciliation. You rejected the Author of Life.'

"I said to them, 'All of heaven watched and observed with sadness and indignation at how you treated the Son of Man, who we have always known in glory, as the Lord, The King of Glory.'

---

[181] Mathew 12:42
[182] Mathew 12:42

"I stood before God's Throne and said to them, 'You religious leaders, Pharisees and Sadducees, you put your fingers in your ears and refused to listen to God's one and only Son. His words were upright and true, and they have finally come to fulfillment on this great day. For He said, [183]'The good man brings good things out of the good stored up in him, and the evil man brings evil things out of the evil stored up in him.' But I tell you that men will have to give account on the Day of Judgment for every careless word they have spoken. For by your words you will be acquitted, and by your words you will be condemned.'"

Moses said, "They said many horrible, wicked and evil things. Their words were like arrows and they had every intention to pierce the Shepherd with the words that flowed from their mouths. The day of reckoning had finally come upon them."

Sheba continued, "I remembered the Pharisees' words burning in me like a fire and these words came out of me like a flood, 'I have heard, all the angels in heaven have heard, all the heavenly hosts have heard and most of all Our Heavenly Father has heard, all that you said about God's one and only Son, The Lord Jesus Christ. What a horrible and terrible thing you have said, what evil has latched upon your hearts!' "Before I could say another word, God the Father stood up and said, [184]"What you have said in the dark will now be heard in the daylight, and what you have whispered in the ear in the inner rooms will now be proclaimed from the rooftops. The books are now open, and what was said has been recorded in the heavenly records, for every word and deed will be proclaimed now for all to hear and judge.'"

Jonathan said, "I remember seconds later that huge mist appeared out of nowhere in front of the great assembly and every eye could see it clearly.

I remember watching as an image slowly came into view

---

[183] Matthew 12:35-37
[184] Luke 12:3

upon the mist. I watched as it became clearer that it was the Angel Gabriel, and he was speaking to someone who I could not see yet in the mist."

Sheba responded, "Yes, we all watched as Gabriel said, [185]'Greetings, you who are highly favored! The Lord is with you. Do not be afraid, Mary, for you have found favor with God. You will be with child and give birth to a son, and you are to give him the name Jesus. He will be great and will be called the Son of the Most High. The Lord God will give Him the throne of His father, David. He will reign over the house of Jacob forever and His kingdom will never end.'

"Then the mist slowly faded and disappeared only for another image to come forward.

"Every eye watched as an image of shepherds materialized in the mist. The shepherds were [186]out in the field keeping watch over their flocks at night. Then angels of the Lord appeared to them, and the glory of the Lord shone around them and everyone could see that they were terrified. They listened to the angel of the Lord say, 'Do not be afraid. I bring you good news of great joy that will be for all the people. Today, in the town of David, a Savior has been born to you; He is Christ the Lord.'"

Jonathan said, "You know, I have seen many Christmas cards in my day with those images, but I never really stopped to consider their significance. I remember hearing Christmas music of great hymns of the faith and they had no impact on my life before I was saved. So many people were exposed to these same images, yet it was like our eyes were closed and we were blind to the most significant event in all of history."

Sheba said, "I watched as many scenes came and faded. One particular scene stands out, I remember watching the [187]heavens

---

[185] Luke 1:26-38
[186] Luke 2:8-15
[187] Luke 3:21-22

open upon Jesus and the Holy Spirit descending on Him in bodily form, much like a dove.'"

Robert said, 'I remember how that image seemed to freeze and   the mist turned to ice and time seemed to stand still. Then everyone watched the Great King stand up and say with a load voice that penetrated every heart and shook the depths of every soul, 'This is my Son, whom I love; with Him I am well pleased.'"

Moses said, "I remember how the Spirit moved among the saints, cheers came forth from every tongue of the redeemed, but one could only here moans, groans and deep cries of anguish from the people before the Throne. All of them knew they had rejected the Son, they feared and dreaded what they knew would come upon them.

"The Great King sat down again and every eye watched as the next scene unfolded.

"That scene showed [209]Jesus standing in a synagogue in Nazareth. He was unrolling a scroll from the prophet Isaiah, and He said, 'The Spirit of the Lord is on me, because He has anointed me to preach good news to the poor. He has sent me to proclaim freedom for the prisoners and recovery of sight for the blind, to release the oppressed, to proclaim the year of the Lord's favor.' We watched Him roll up the scroll, give it back to the attendant and sit down. And the eyes of everyone in the synagogue were fastened on Him as He said, 'Today, this Scripture is fulfilled in your hearing.'"

"Those are such beautiful words that were said, words of freedom for the prisoners, enlightenment for the blind, and relief for the oppressed. Many times, I dreamed of saying those same words, but I was afraid that the people that the Lord put in my path would not respond to them. I knew these words were the way to freedom, but I did very little with them," Jonathan added.

Sheba continued, "I watched as another scene appeared in the mist and I saw [210]Jesus walking beside the Sea of Galilee, then up the side   of a mountain where He then sat down. Great crowds came to Him bringing the lame, the blind, the crippled, the mute and many others, and they laid them at His feet; and Jesus healed them all."

"They had so many miracles; I never realized how many Jesus did until all those scenes unfolded before me. Seeing the mute healed and speaking, the crippled made well and walking, the blind seeing and the dead rising were amazing." Jonathan added.

Robert added, "It was so beautiful to see the great mercy and compassion of our King being poured out on the helpless, the lost, the widowed, the fatherless and the downcast. My heart was captured and my spirit delighted at the work of His hands."

Moses spoke. "I remember when those other scenes began unfolding, scenes of rejection and humiliation by the people of that generation. One scene in particular burned in my heart that day when a [188]demon-possessed man who was blind and mute was brought to Jesus and He healed him so that he could both talk and see. I saw that all the people were astonished and said, 'Could this be the Son of David?' I remember watching and hearing in disbelief as the Pharisees said, [189]'It is only by Beelzebub, the prince of demons that He drives out demons.'"

"I also remember how the whole assembly of the saints raised their voices in protest," Robert added.

Sheba continued, "The next scene began to appear and it showed Jesus in a synagogue and a man with a shriveled hand was there. Jesus said to the man [190]'Stretch out your hand,' so he stretched it out and it was completely restored, looking just like the other.

"That is when the Lord moved in me and I pointed at the Pharisees, Sadducees and the men of that generation and said, 'Look at these men. Instead of acknowledging the miracle, the mercy that was shown to that helpless man, instead of praising God these wicked men became [191]furious and began to plot with one another

---

[188] Matthew 12:22-24
[189] Matthew 9:34
[190] Matthew 12:13-14
[191] Mark 3:5-6

how they might kill Jesus.'"

Robert said, "I remember when you spoke next your voice was louder and even more convicting. It echoed throughout the whole assembly as you laid charges against them. You said, 'These wicked men were jealous. Consider their own words carefully!' then another scene materialized showing a meeting of the chief priests and the elders of the people. And they said, [192]'What are we accomplishing here? This man is performing many signs. If we let Him go on like this, everyone will believe in Him, and then the Romans will come and take away both our temple and our nation.' Then Caiaphas the High Priest said 'You know nothing at all! You do not realize that it is better for you that one man dies for the people than that the whole nation perishes.'"

Moses added with a voice of disdain, "I remember the glee on their faces when Judas entered into their courts. They were so willing and delighted to give him money in exchange for Jesus' life. I remember watching the money exchanging hands and Judas taking the thirty pieces of silver."

Sheba continued, "I watched as the next scene began to appear on the mist. I saw the fig trees and then an olive grove appeared and I watched as my Lord said, [193]'My soul is overwhelmed with sorrow to the point of death.'

"I watched as He fell to the ground and prayed again, 'My Father, if it is possible, may this cup be taken from me. Yet not as I will, but as you will.'

"I watched as He prayed a second time, 'My Father, if it is not possible for this cup to be taken away unless I drink it, may your will be done.'

Robert replied, "The silence at that moment was deafening. Everyone knew what was going to happen next, and we

[192] John 11:48-49
[193] Matthew 26:4-5, 28:38-32

watched as [194]Judas arrived with a large crowd armed with swords and clubs.

"We all watched as Judas whisper to the guards, 'The one I kiss is the man; arrest him,' and he walked over to Jesus and said, 'Greetings, Rabbi!' and kissed him. Jesus replied, 'Friend, do what you came for.'

"I was speechless as I watched the men go over, seize Jesus and arrest Him. Then one of Jesus' companions reached for his sword, drew it out and struck the servant of the high priest, cutting off his ear. 'Put your sword back in its place,' Jesus said to him, 'For all who draw the sword will die by the sword. Do you think I cannot call on my Father, and He will at once put at my disposal more than twelve legions of angels?'"

Jonathan said, "It was surprising and amazing at that point to see twelve legions of angels, twelve thousand angels flying in from every direction of the Judgment Hall and rushing to the Lord's side, to carry out His commands, to show their allegiance to the Lord Jesus Christ. I remember them standing before the Throne and waiting for His command. We all knew why they were there, to bind and chain that generation and carry them away into the outer darkness, where there would be weeping and gnashing of teeth."

Sheba said, "I stood there that day, unaware of the scenes and what would be shown. I was not worried, for the Lord's words were written on my heart. He said to me, [218]'Do not worry about what to say or how to say it. At that time, you will be given what to say, for it will not be you speaking, but the Spirit of your Father speaking through you.'

"So, I watched as the next scene came into view. Jesus was standing before [219]Caiaphas, the High Priest, the teachers of the law, the elders, the chief priests and the whole Sanhedrin were

---

[194] Matthew 26:47-56

there looking for false evidence against Jesus so that they could put him to death. But they did not find any, even though many false witnesses came forward.

"I watched as two people came forward and declared, 'This fellow said, I am able to destroy the temple of God and rebuild it in three days.'

"Then I watched as the High Priest said, 'I charge you under oath by the living God: Tell us if you are the Christ, the Son of God?'

"The scene froze and excitement began to build up. Finally, Jesus said, 'Yes, it is as you say, but I say to all of you: In the future you will see the Son of Man sitting at the right hand of the Mighty One and coming on the clouds of Heaven.'

"Instantaneously, the Heavenly Host and all the redeemed cheered and applause broke out all over the great assembly. His word came to fulfillment for every eye saw Him, even those who pierced Him.

"They watched as the High Priest tore his clothes and said, 'He has spoken blasphemy! Why do we need any more witnesses? Look, now you have heard the blasphemy. What do you think?' '"He is worthy of death,' they answered.

"Everyone watched scenes unfolded before them. Every tongue was silent as they spit upon Jesus' face and struck Him with their fists. And they watched as others slapped Him and said, 'Prophesy to us, Christ. Who hit you?'"

Jonathan spoke up, "I remember watching and hearing every hit and slap. It was like I was there. With every slap and hit I felt emotions deep down in my soul. I was furious, filled with sadness, filled with mixed emotions all at the same time. I felt like turning away, but I could not. I hated to see Him endure such pain and humiliation from sinful men, even though He did it for me; it made my heart break."

Moses said, "I believe God wanted us to feel the pain, or

should I say the effects of the blows deep in our hearts to show us that He has an immense love for us, and us for Him. He was showing us that we were, and are, affected by everything He did for us."

Robert said, "It is almost like in Romans where it said we were baptized with Him in His death."

Sheba continued, "I said to the great congregation, 'You have seen and heard the beating He endured. It echoed in our ears and every strike seemed to hit our souls. Look how they treated our Lord. Look even now as another scene unfolds. Watch as they bring our Lord before the Gentiles, before Pilate. See them lay the charges against Him and see how even Pilate saw through their hypocrisy and tried to let Him go.

We all watched [220]as the Chief Priest and the elders persuaded the crowd to ask for Barabbas in exchange for our Lord, and they persuaded the crowd to have Him executed.

"Everyone that day heard the crowds yell out, 'Crucify him! Crucify him!'

"Remember the last words before our Lord was beaten and ridiculed, Pilate said, 'I am innocent of this man's blood, it is your responsibility!' And they answered 'Let his blood be on us and on our children!' Then they released Barabbas to them. But they handed over our Lord, the King of Glory, to be flogged and to be crucified upon the cross."

Jonathan said, "I remember at that point there was a silence for a time, and everyone waited to see what was going to happen next. Then the Lord stood up and called forth a great host of men and they came out of nowhere."

Moses replied, "Yes, Jesus said that [195]the men of Nineveh would rise up and condemn that generation. They acknowledged that they repented at the preaching of Jonah. And the men of Nineveh all said in unison, 'This generation is guilty, for one

---

[195] Matthew 12:41

even greater than Jonah came to you and you did not accept His testimony and turn in repentance.'"

Robert added, "I remember the whole assembly cried out, 'Guilty, guilty.'"

Sheba said, "One of the final scenes was the Crucifixion of the Lord. I remember as the scene began, a man came forward before the throne and faced the great assembly and began to open a weathered looking scroll, he unrolled it before everyone and said as the crucifixion was happening,

"'Who has believed our message, and to whom has the arm of the Lord been revealed? He was despised and rejected by men, a man of sorrows, and familiar with suffering. Like one from whom men hide their faces. He was despised, and we esteemed Him not. He was oppressed and afflicted; yet He did not open His mouth. He was led like a lamb to the slaughter. As a sheep before her shearers is silent, so He did not open His mouth. By oppression and judgment, He was taken away. And who can speak of His descendants? For He was cut off from the land of the living; He was assigned a grave with the wicked and with the rich in His death, though He had done no violence, nor was any deceit in His mouth.'

"At the end of the passage the man rolled up the scroll. No one had to ask who the man was, for everyone knew he was the prophet Isaiah." Sheba said to the small group, "And we all know how it ended for that generation, when the final passage was read against them, but not by me."

Chapter 20: The King's Judgment

The Great King stood up in splendor and majesty and confronted those before the throne.

"Woe to you, teachers of the law and Pharisees, you hypocrites! You are like whitewashed tombs which look beautiful on the outside but on the inside are full of dead men's bones and everything unclean.

"In the same way, on the outside you appear to people as righteous, but on the inside, you are full of hypocrisy and wickedness.

"Woe to you, teachers of the law and Pharisees, you hypocrites! You build tombs for the prophets and decorate the graves of the righteous. And you say, 'If we had lived in the days of our forefathers, we would not have taken part with them in shedding the blood of the prophets.' So, you testify against yourselves that you are the descendants of those who murdered the prophets. Fill up, then, the measure of the sin of your forefathers!"

"You snakes! You brood of vipers! You will not escape being condemned to Hell. In the past I have sent you prophets and wise men and teachers. Some of them you killed and crucified; others you flogged in your synagogues and pursued from town to town. And so upon you will come all the righteous blood that has been shed on earth, from the righteous blood of Abel to the blood of Zechariah, son of Berekiah, whom you murdered between the temple and the altar. I tell you the truth; all this has now come upon you today on this generation."

Moses added, "At that point, the place was silenced; a pin could have been heard if it fell. The only thing that could be heard was the people in front of the throne, where there was shuddering, moaning and weeping."

"Then, the Great King said with a voice that

thundered, [196]"Depart from me, you who are cursed, into the eternal fire prepared for the devil and his angels.'

"The entire place was silenced as the mighty angels flew down upon them and the cries could be heard as they were brought away to the place where they did not want to go."

After this was said, the small group was silenced as they remembered that day and the judgments that fell upon the whole world. Jonathan was the first to speak and said, "That day was filled with mixed emotions. I remember being sad because they rejected the only Savior given to man, and happy because righteousness was finally shining like stars and we were accepted as heirs of the kingdom. They had so many charges laid against them; they only [197]valued the worth of our Lord's life at thirty pieces of silver. Praise God that others see Him as a treasure and a pearl of great price.

Robert spoke next and said, "It was amazing how our Lord's Judgment was so complete. He was able to call every generation to account. He judged not only the individual's life, but how that individual life affected the world they lived in. He examined how each individual life affected their neighborhoods, cities and countries. On that day, all mankind had fallen very short!"

Jonathan said, "I can see in my own life, sadly enough, that I did not influence my generation the way I should have, or even the people I knew and loved. In hindsight, I could have done so much more, but the Spirit is willing and the flesh is weak."

Sheba said, "That's all I have to say for now."

Suddenly a bright light enveloped them and the Lord Jesus in all His glory appeared in the midst of the little group sitting in the alcove.

He said, "A lot has been said, and I want to reveal even more mysteries, things hidden before the foundations of the

---

[196] Matthew 25:41
[197] Zachariah 11:13

world."

The little group brightened up and waited with great expectation, which was visible on each face.

Jesus said to them, "You have seen every living human being stand before me. For it was said, [198]For we must all appear before the Judgment Seat of Christ, that each one may receive what is due him for the things done while in the body, whether good or bad.

"In the Old World, many of your brothers, sisters and others have raised this question throughout the ages: 'Is it fair for God to judge the man who lives in the remotest parts of the world, who has not heard the Gospel, the Good News?'

"To begin, many asked this sincerely because they were seeking truth and they wondered how my eternal plans could be played out. Others asked this question to cause debate, and others raised this question in accusatory manner. They were questioning my Father's character and His ability to judge righteously.

"I am the Creator, does it not say that [199]I created all things: things in Heaven and on Earth, visible and invisible, whether thrones or powers or rulers or authorities; all things were created by me and for me? That I was before all things, and in me all things hold together? And that I am the head of the body, the church; I am also the beginning and the firstborn from among the dead, so that in everything I might have the supremacy? If I am the Creator, would I not know where every man is and the circumstances he is in?

"I am not only the Creator, but also the Sustainer of everything that exists. [200]I laid the earth's foundation, marked off its dimensions, set earth's footings in place. I set the seas in its place and fixed limits for it and said, 'This far you may come and no farther; here is where you proud waves halt! I cut a channel for the

---

[198] 2 Corinthians 5:10
[199] Colossians 1:15-18
[200] Job 38

torrents of rain and set the paths for the thunderstorms to water the land where no man lives, a desert with no one living in it, to satisfy a desolate wasteland and make the grass grow.

"I not only control the Earth, but the heavens also. I alone can bind the beautiful Pleiades and loose the cords of Orion and bring forth the constellations in their seasons. I also set and know the laws of the heavens and setup my dominion over the earth.

"It is I who sustains every human being, as Job's friend Elihu said of me, [201]'If it were His intention and He withdrew His spirit and breath, all mankind would perish together and man would return to the dust from which he came.'

"It is by my hands, my will and my desire that all the heavens and the Earth did not roll up like a scroll until the appointed time. I know every man, and what is in every man, not one of them kept themselves alive, but I sustained them.

"Do I not fill the universe? [202]Where can you flee from my Spirit? Where can someone go to escape my presence? If they go up to the heavens, I am there; if they make their bed in the depths, I am there. If they were to rise on the wings of the dawn and settle on the far side of the sea, even there my hands guide them and my right hand will hold them fast.

"Do I not control all things? Do I not control the [203]lightning and hail, snow and clouds, storms and winds; do they not do my bidding? [204]In my Temple come flashes of lightning, rumblings, peals of thunder, earthquakes and great hailstorms are seen. [205]I make the clouds my chariot and I ride on the wings of the wind. I make winds my messengers and flames of fire my servants.

"Do I not control all mankind and move them for my

---

[201] Job 34:14-15
[202] Psalm 139:7-10
[203] Psalm 148:8
[204] Revelation 11:19
[205] Psalm 104:3-4

good purposes? [206]From one man I made all the nations, that they should inhabit the whole earth; and I marked out their appointed times in history and the boundaries of their lands. I did this so that they would seek me and perhaps reach out for me and find me, though I was not far from any one of them. For in me, you lived and moved and had your being. "If I am everywhere, and can I not move all things according to my good purpose? If I control the whirlwinds and the storms, and if I feed all the animals when I open my hands, would I not be aware of all the people who dwelt upon the earth? Yes, I know all men, I know what is in everyman and I know where every man lived throughout the ages.

"I have revealed myself to all men in many ways, for I am the Creator and the Sustainer of all things, and I have always left myself with a witness upon the earth. Let's go to the Celestial Sea and discuss these things and you will see that I have reached out and shown my love to all of creation."

---

[206] Acts 17:26-31

Chapter 21: God's Loving Testimony

They all left the little alcove and walked back toward the River of Life. Once they reached the river, they followed it down-stream walking upon the cobblestone streets of pure gold that followed adjacent to the river.

The buildings on each side of them alternated in color from tan to red and white. They were all about three or four stories high with beautiful wrought iron balconies on each floor. On the first floor, many of the doors were open and various tables were set for people to gather together and visit. Palm trees ran down each side of the street about twenty feet apart. Every mile or so, there was a break in the buildings to make way for a large circular park in which the road would split and curve around on each side and join together on the opposite end.

Many people were walking down the streets. As they passed by, the saints would bow to the Lord. On many occasions the Lord would stop to talk to someone and then depart giving them a smile, a hug or even a gift. Jonathan watched on one of these occasions when the Lord gave a woman a white stone with words engraved in gold upon it. He could not read what was said, but the excitement that broke upon her face showed that it spoke volumes to her soul.

They continued to walk past thousands of people in joyful assembly. Other people joined their group as they walked, and the small group continued to grow to about five thousand people. As the Lord walked, He would gesture to someone to come along. Others came out of buildings and parks they passed, and Jonathan could tell that the Lord called them to their group in some special way.

They finally reached the sea where part of the River of Life branched out and emptied into it. They walked upon a beach that was a few hundred yards wide and continued on into the horizon. They finally reached an area with a high hill, and Jesus walked up, sat on top of the hill and every one gathered below in groups of ten, twenty, fifty and a hundred. Then He raised His hands to quiet the crowd and began to speak.

"Welcome my beloved, my faithful ones. I called you here to teach you how I showed love to all of my creation. I want you to understand how I reached out my loving hands, even to the disobedient. My love and my grace extended to the ends of the earth, and I would like to explain the various ways in which I did this.

"To begin with, the heavens declared my glory and the sky proclaimed the work of my hands. [207]Day after day my creation cried out, and night after night they revealed knowledge. They had no speech and they used no words and no sound could be heard, yet creation's voice went out into the entire world. Their words spread to the ends of the earth."

As He said these words, something like a canopy appeared in the heavens above, and it covered the entire area. At first it was black, and then stars began to appear in increasing brightness until it covered the entire canopy. Then, the moon seemed to rise and arch its way to the center of the canopy. As they looked, it became apparent it was the old universe and all the constellations were visible.

As the Lord spoke, the stars sparkled in the sky above them and everyone was filled with awe as they looked upon the beauty of the old creation, they had taken for granted. Galaxies and constellations were also brought forth at certain times as He spoke. Each one displayed their individual glory; it was as if the stars themselves were on stage, bowing before the Lord, as they shone forth and revealed the God of all creation.

"My creation was plain to all men, and there was sufficient evidence for all men to know that a gracious loving God created all these things. I loved beauty, and I knew my creation would love beauty also, so out of a great love I filled all of my creation with wonderful colors to display my joy and love for all

---

[207] Psalm 19:1-3

mankind. I created a world that could be enjoyed, appreciated and loved. That creation was a signpost that pointed back to many of your heavenly Father's attributes.

"Consider the beauty of the forest. I made all kinds of trees grow, trees that were pleasing to the eye and good for food to satisfy the hearts of man. Consider the flowers that shine forth their glory every spring and how they beautify the landscape. Their smell and fragrance are carried on the breeze into everyone's nostrils, exciting the senses and showing that the winter is over. Life springs up everywhere, the brown grass becomes green, the barren trees begin to bud, and various colors and shaped leaves bloom showing their glory. I did not make a grey earth with grey grass and trees, but I made an earth that is rich in color and pleasing to the eye. All of creation points to your heavenly Father's love for all of mankind."

As the Lord spoke, trees and flowers of every kind burst forth from the ground all around them, and the variety of smells fell upon them, all their wonderful fragrances captivating the group. Everyone was amazed as they gazed upon the beauty of the old creation, they had looked past in the old world. That part of creation also took the stage and bowed before the Lord as they displayed the glory of the God of all creation.

"My creation was plain to all men, and there was sufficient evidence for all men to know that a gracious loving God created all these things.

"Consider the rich variety of food that has been created, from the various fruits and vegetables with their various shapes, sizes and colors. Your heavenly Father created all these flavors to satisfy and bring joy to the hearts of men. These also were signposts pointing to a loving and caring creator."

As He said this, various tastes touched the palette of every tongue so that they could experience all the variety of God's goodness.

"Consider the fish and all the other creatures that inhabit the streams, ponds, lakes and oceans. So many varieties of colors and beauty all created to excite the heart of man, and yet no man who ever lived tasted all the bounty that the Lord created to satisfy the hearts of man.

"I filled the whole world with a rich variety of my grace. Consider all the beautiful animals from the dove to the peacock, from the kitten to the majestic lion, from the tropical fish to the various whales. All these things were made to give man a variety of pleasure and all these things displayed your heavenly Father's loving-kindness.

"So I say to you today, [208]since the creation of the world, God's invisible qualities, His eternal power and divine nature have been clearly seen and understood from what has been made so that men are without excuse. For by creation they knew God, but neither thanked Him nor glorified Him.

"I have also written my laws on the heart of every man so that the world would not fall into utter chaos and destruction. I gave man a conscience to know right from wrong. I kept man's wickedness in check, [209]though many have seared their conscience as with a hot iron. I kept many people safe by giving authority to the governing bodies to protect the innocent from the schemes of wicked men. I put the [210]authorities in place, also, as my servants to do well and to administer justice. They are my servants, agents of wrath to bring punishment to the lawbreakers, for they do not bear the sword for nothing.

"I protected the world from the ravages of sin, though it permeated the very depths of man's heart. My Spirit fought against the flood of sin from the very beginning; for if sin was left unchecked, it would have ravaged the whole world and made life unbearable. Man's wickedness would continue to grow if it was left unchecked. I wanted love and peace to abound, so I created the conscience to govern man. My Spirit also strived to stop the flood of pain and

---

[208] Romans 1:20-21
[209] 1 Timothy 4:2
[210] Romans 13:4

misery that would have consumed the whole world.

This, also, is an example of my love. "Consider my love for all men. I sent you, my beloved, into [211]the whole world to make disciples of all nations, baptizing them in the name of the Father, the Son and the Holy Spirit, teaching them to obey everything I have commanded. [212]I was not willing that any should perish, but that all would come to repentance. So, I made you, my church, a light in a very dark world. I reached out my hand of salvation to all men, people from every nation, race and culture.

[213] "You see, at just the right time, when you were still powerless, I died for the ungodly. Very rarely will anyone die for a righteous person, though for a good person someone might possibly dare to die. But I demonstrated my own love for you in this: While you were still sinners, I laid my life down for you.

"My love was demonstrated on the cross for all men to see, and by my resurrection I opened the door to eternal life. I didn't just ask people to repent, but [214]God also commanded people everywhere to repent. [215]I have declared to both Jews and Greeks that they must turn to God in repentance and have faith in our Lord Jesus. So [216]I commanded all people to repent and turn to God so that their sins may be wiped out, so times of refreshing may come from the Lord.

"Where the gospel was not proclaimed by mouth, I sent my word in many diverse manners. I have sent missionaries and evangelists into the farthest parts of the world, and even though many did not hear their words, their testimonies and their Bibles were left behind so that all people could hear my words. The gospel

---

[211] Matthew 28:19-20
[212] 2 Peter 3:9
[213] Romans 5:6-8
[214] Act 17:30-31
[215] Acts 20:21
[216] Acts 3:19

has been proclaimed to all men, to every creation under Heaven, so that they are without excuse.

"I also know what is in all men, and I can overcome every barrier in every man. I can overcome man's stubbornness. I can overcome their fear of the light that their deeds may be exposed. I can overcome all the works of Satan because I am the Strong Man that holds him back. I am above all and in all. Nothing can hold my hand back from where I desire to place it.

"I have made man unique in all of creation. He is different than all the animals for he is made in my image and after my likeness. I have made man eternal so that I can have an eternal relationship with them. I gave them the ability to communicate so that they can know my will. I gave them the ability to reason so that they can serve me in unique ways. I gave them the ability to worship me with their whole heart so that they can feel my presence and love. I gave them a soul so that they can worship me in spirit and in truth. I have given them a mind so that they can think and reason on how they can worship and know me better.

"I have not treated the rest of creations like this, for they are temporal, unique from man; man is a living, spiritual being made in my image and made for a special relationship with me.

"So, you are all here today for you came to me to have life, and have it to the fullest. I am the everlasting life and streams of water flow from within me, and you have all drunk from that fountain from where the wells of salvation flow. I have freely given so that you would also freely give to each other and continue to love and serve each other.

"Always be ready to worship and to serve. Consider always the rock from which you were hewn, for I am the first of the resurrected and you followed. It was always my desire to share, not only my home with you, but my life as well. So, as I am the Bread of Life, I give to you some of the hidden manna." As He said this, the twelve apostles came over the rise of the hill where Jesus sat and He blessed the food and gave it   to the twelve and they passed it out among the crowd.

They all ate and they were all satisfied. When they were through eating, there were twelve baskets full of left overs. About five thousand people were fed there that day. When they were all through, Jesus then stood up, lifted up His hands and blessed the people and sent them on their way.

As Jonathan was on his way home, a man ran up beside him and said excitedly, "Hi Jonathan, the Lord told me to introduce myself to you so that we could get to know each other. My name is Epaphras."

"Hello Epaphras," Jonathan said as he turned toward him. "It's a pleasure to meet you," he said with great joy.

Jonathan started laughing as he asked in a very monotone voice, "Where are you from, and what century did you live in?"

Epaphras laughed and said, "I've heard that question a few thousand times."

"I was from Colossae, which was about twelve miles from Laodicea, and I lived in the early first century." He said with a smile.

"Did you know any of the people mentioned in the Scriptures?" "I knew a few of them: Justus, Luke, Demas, Nympha and Paul."

"The only ones I heard of were Luke and Paul, if they are the same Luke and Paul mentioned in the Bible," Jonathan said.

"They are the same ones, the Apostle Paul and Luke, the Doctor who wrote the Book of Luke. I knew them well, and I also knew Justin, Demas and Nympha, who are also mentioned in the scriptures," Epaphras added.

Because he had never heard of them, Jonathan noted that he should look them up in the Scriptures later.

Epaphras added, "I was briefly mentioned in Scripture too, but that is not important."

Jonathan's head turned quickly as he said, "You were? Where? [217]Epaphras chuckled and answered, "Colossians and Philemon."

Jonathan started racking his memory trying to find some clue as to who this man might be.

Epaphras said, "Let's go to the place where they had the Wedding Feast of the Lamb and we can talk there."

As they started toward the center of the kingdom, Epaphras began humming a very familiar song.

"If you want to be great in God's Kingdom, learn to be the servant of all."

Jonathan's thoughts shot back to the beautiful house he saw on the city's main street. He remembered Jesus saying that it was one of the most beautiful homes in the entire kingdom, and yet this person was not well known on earth, but His light shined brightly through him to his generation.

A smile fell upon Jonathan's face as he walked with Epaphras; the Conversations started as they walked down the streets of gold in the celestial city.

Let the reader remember this, that [218]Jesus performed many other signs and miracles in the presence of His people which are not recorded in this book. But these are written that you may believe that Jesus is the Messiah, the Son of God, and that by believing you may have life in His name.

---

[217] Epaphras is mentioned in Colossians 1:7, 4:12-13, Philippians 1:23
[218] John 20:30

1 Corinthians 2:9-10,

"No eye has seen, no ear has heard, no mind has conceived what God has prepared for those who love him-these are the things God has revealed to us by his Spirit."

About the Author

Alan Duprey was born in Holyoke, Massachusetts. He graduated from the Machine Shop program at Holyoke Trade School. After high school, he enlisted in the United States Navy as a machinist. After an honorable discharge, he attended Springfield Technical Community College in Massachusetts following the drafting and design program. He also attended Westfield State College completing the teaching certification program for teaching in Vocational Schools.

He now resides in Agawam, Massachusetts. He has been happily married to his wife, Jennie, since 1987. He has two children. He has been a machinist most of his life and was a machine shop instructor at William J. Dean Technical/Vocational High School. After seven years, he left the Vocational School and started teaching Mastercam CAD-CAM software at MACDAC Engineering. He then purchased the company with his brother and has been part owner of the company since 2002. His duties include Mastercam sales and demonstrations showing the software's capabilities throughout New England.

He came to faith in the Lord Jesus Christ in 1988 through New Life Presbyterian Church (OPC). He attends Christ Community Church in Belchertown, MA. Over the years, he has taught Bible studies, Sunday school, small groups, men's study and has filled the pulpit when needed. This is his first book and he is waiting to see if the Lord is opening a door for writing a series of books with the same character.